PAY IT FORWARD

by M Novak

Prologue

I heard someone say once that you can just stop at a certain age. Stop progressing. Stop developing. Stop moving forward. A traumatic event can precipitate this phenomenon. That's what happened to me. I reached the age of twenty and then I stayed there. I am still twenty.

My name is Abby.

Chapter 1

There is a junction on the Autopista del Sol running between Mexico City and Acapulco where it is possible to get distracted and make a wrong turn. Unfortunately, that turn is extremely wrong, dangerously wrong. I had no idea about any of this before I arrived in Mexico, or even whilst I was there. I only found out when it was too late.

I went to Mexico in the November of my gap year directly after my birthday. I had spent the months since finishing my A-levels working in an upmarket restaurant, in an expensive area far from my own home. It served pretentious, fussy dishes like rabbit paella and lobster. My dad found it hilarious and always asked me to bring some home, but when I did, he would looked at it perplexed and we'd end up throwing it away.

I only got the job because I was pretty. I knew that at the time and I know that now. The difference is that at the time I took it for granted. I presumed that that was how the world would work for me.

All through my childhood, things had happened for me because I was pretty. I got picked to be the lead in school plays every year, even though I couldn't act. Teachers would rest their eyes on me smiling in relief, as if I was special. I got away with petty misdemeanours that others didn't.

Consequently, girls never liked me much. They would invent nasty character traits for me and use them as justifications to dislike me, but that was a lie. They didn't like me because I was attractive, that was the truth of it.

Back then, being desirable was one of the main functions of a female. Not so much anymore, I know. Nowadays, there is much more talk of having a great character, of girls having brains. Back then, it was all about snagging a husband with a decent job. That's all the previous generation would go on about, that's all we heard growing up. Ergo, when boys came onto the scene, it was even worse for me. All the haters really came out of the woodwork then, in a massive way.

Weird rumours would be invented about me all the time. Mainly about promiscuous things I was supposed to have done with boys at parties or in the undergrowth at the local park. I tried to laugh at the absurdity of these accusations. Literally, all I did was go to school and either go home or go to work.

I started to work really young because my family, as I said, was not well off. At fourteen, I started to babysit. I picked up this little kid who was at the primary school located next to my secondary school, and I looked after her until her parents got home at around seven. That was my life.

No boys. No parties. No misbehaviour.

That went on for years and then when I was old enough, I got a job at a local Italian restaurant. I worked every shift going, for peanuts. They appeared to be kind people, but really, they were stingy. At one point, I was babysitting and waitressing at the same time. I would often be falling asleep on my desk at school, especially if the classroom was overheated, as it frequently was.

Yet, still I got the haters ganging up on me, huddling in their mean little groups and giving me the side-eye. Even if I'd had the chance or the time, I would never have done any of the things that I was rumoured to have done. I didn't fancy their spotty, scrawny boyfriends, not one little bit. Also, and most significantly, I was nowhere near them; I was always at work. Their hatred of me was not evidence-based however, it was visceral. I was always tense and anxious, waiting for some petty attack, not full-blown violence, you understand, just some minor nastiness, just about minor enough to be considered an example of malicious horseplay and to avoid serious repercussions.

For example, a couple of times I would be on the bus and when I got home, I realised that someone had put chewing gum in my long hair. I couldn't prove anything, but I knew that it was one of them. If I was ever stupid enough to leave my school bag lying somewhere, unattended, I could pretty much guarantee that something would have been taken. Often, it would be something small which would nevertheless get me into trouble, like a maths geometry set. Having said that, I also mysteriously lost three calculators and those were expensive at the time. Almost every day, I would enter a classroom and 'Abby is a slapper' or something similar would be scrawled across the blackboard. I learnt to ignore it completely and the teachers always pretended that nothing was amiss. They'd just erase it without comment and get on with the lesson. Noone ever considered my feelings.

People didn't make so much of feelings back then. Funnily enough, I got on well with my parents, but I wouldn't have dreamt of telling them about any of the minor bullying instances. I was supposed to stand up for myself. We all were.

I did OK in my A-levels, not brilliantly, just OK. Being pretty couldn't help me with those. However, by the time I received the results, I knew where I was going to university anyway. It was a sure thing as soon as they invited me for an interview and I realised that the interview was being conducted by a man.

Of course, I got an unconditional offer to study English at Penbridge, a beautiful campus- based university in the remote North West. Other kids with much better results did not get offers. For this too, I was hated.

So, at eighteen, this is what I looked like: I was tall and slim and curvy all at once. I had this long shiny chestnut hair which looked as if it should be in a commercial, enormous brown eyes, a tiny nose and full lips. I was forever getting asked if I was a model. It got on my nerves, the constant attention. There was a significant drawback though. As you have probably deduced by now, I didn't have many friends. Only Emma and Zoe really and only because, if I'm being honest, we went to primary school together and our families knew each other.

We all used to hang out together when we were small. We had playdates and barbecues and Halloween parties at each other's houses, well mine and Emma's houses. I don't think they liked me much then either. Maybe I was a bit mean to them, I don't really remember. I think I was a bit confused. So many people were nasty to me that I never expected anyone to be kind or friendly, especially not anyone of my age. Our mums even had a book club together at some point, even though none of them were readers. I think it was just an excuse to drink wine and gossip.

Anyway, both Emma and Zoe attended the same secondary school as I did and we still kind of hung out together, sometimes. I always suspected that they saw more of each other without me. There were lots of shared references which were nothing to do with me, a bit like a secret language. Still, I had a lot going on with all the bitchiness aimed at me and all my jobs. It is true that I did always have a little posse of boys following me around and trying to talk to me. That was not my fault though, I didn't encourage it, whatever people said.

Emma was smart too, really brainy. Top university type brainy. She didn't seem to care for boys at all, didn't even seem to notice them. Zoe was just kind of average. Emma's unofficial sidekick; she was shy, very introverted actually, and a bit chubby. She was nowhere near as clever as Emma but worked too hard. You know the type, a bit worried.

There was some kind of issue in Zoe's family that I never got to the bottom of. Her parents were both there, but barely. It was an unhappy house. That is what it felt like. Cold. Whenever we went there, which was extremely rarely, we felt uncomfortable. The surfaces were hard and unyielding. The atmosphere was weird, unpleasant. We would sit in her room or in the living room and it just felt kind of pointless, you know? Like a waste of time when we could be someplace better. We'd feel guilty though, a sinking in the chest, because you could tell that Zoe wanted us to be there. Especially Emma, she definitely wanted Emma to be there.

Also, she had this brother, Paul, who was extremely annoying. He was only a year younger but still growing in that awkward, pointy way that teenage boys develop. He was always trying to hang out with us and Zoe never told him to bugger off. It was as if she wanted him there, which really irritated me. He would always try and sit next to me and just stared and stared at my face. They looked extremely alike, Zoe and Paul. They had this bright sandy coloured hair which was weird because both parents were kind of mousy and grey. The way their home was you'd think that both kids would be scrappy and mean, but they weren't. Not yet anyway, just a bit odd.

Emma looked a bit like a downgraded version of me. All the right components were there but they didn't quite merge in the perfect way or they were just a little bit off. For instance, her nose had a noticeable bump on it. In addition, she was short, shorter than average, and her bottom was kind of large, before big bottoms became fashionable.

Emma was an only child and her parents adored her. They were so proud of how brainy she was. She was forever winning maths awards and science competitions and her certificates and trophies were everywhere in the house. Like a whole interior decorating scheme devoted to the achievements of Emma. It pissed me off to be honest.

Most of our town was from working class stock. None of our parents were academic. My own brother, Simon, and I were not worshipped. We were just treated as normal kids in a functional type of way. Simon really was a normal kid, an average boy of the era. Two years younger than me, he was mad about football and wrestling and always in trouble for semi-serious fighting in the playground. He looked mischievous, like a naughty elf. He had messy dark hair and his ears stuck out a bit. We got on well when we were young children, before I became a princess.

I know it. I know what I became. I am aware that I thought too much of myself, but in my defence people kind of forced it onto me, this silly status. I got too much negative attention. That was the problem. Too many people were always looking at me. It really wasn't my fault. All the boys fancying me and all the girls, jealous; it twisted something in my brain.

So, in the November of my gap year I flew to Mexico City.

Emma had a Mexican boyfriend, Enrique, whom she had met when he came to England on a two- week residential the year before. They met in a coffee shop and then they continued to meet in a chaste way so that he could 'practise his English'. She didn't want me or Zoe to meet him and we used to tease her about that.

"Why what's wrong with him? Is he hideous?"

Anyway, weirdly, improbably, they kept in touch and she decided to spend her own gap year teaching English in the same city in which he lived. I'm not sure how much serious thought she had given their relationship beforehand, but very quickly after she arrived in September, he did become her proper boyfriend, her first proper boyfriend. I knew that about her. I knew she hadn't ever had a proper boyfriend before. Not even drunk snogging around the back of some church hall or in the murky shadow of some trees. Some boy's freezing hands trailing up your top. She'd never had any of that before.

It was kind of sweet, touching.

Enrique was the real deal and he was the first. She was always eager to stress that he was a rich Mexican. A distinction which was meaningless to me until I got there and observed the glaring blatant disparity between rich and poor all around me.

Emma said that they would collect me from the airport. I was completely disorientated when I arrived. All those hours with my long limbs scrunched up in an economy seat. Walking out into a wall of humidity and pollution. The plane was a bit early. They were a bit late. Either way, I didn't see them at first and then when I did see Emma, I didn't recognise her. She had lost loads of weight and she looked completely different; sophisticated and older. Of course, she had managed to pick up the language straightaway and the two of them were chattering away in Spanish.

When she turned to me, there was a moment, shining plainly on her face, of resentment. She didn't really want me intruding into her brand new world. But it was just a moment before she gathered her features into an acceptable welcome. The boy, Enrique, was tall. At first, all I could see was dark floppy hair and long limbs. Then he turned to me and almost imperceptibly, his eyes swept me up and down. Aha, I thought, here we go.

The thing was, the problem really, was that he was beautiful. Is, no doubt, still beautiful somewhere. Exotic and beautiful. Beautiful like some women are beautiful; the eyes, the lashes, the delicate features and the graceful limbs.

Something melted in me then. It wasn't lust, or not just lust, it was more than that. It was a warmth. It almost felt like nostalgia for something which I had never had.

Chapter 2

Emma rented a flat. It was more of a studio really. It was one large room with a mattress in the corner, sheets dishevelled. It took us a long time to get there. Enrique had a black car, an American car, one that I recognised from films and we drove down interminable highways. Scruffy apartment buildings loomed on the side of the road. There were shops and people everywhere. Elegant districts merged seamlessly into quasi slums, squat huts masquerading as shops. Everywhere the cacophony of traffic, pollution heavy on the lungs, almost immediately, like treacle lining your airways.

I felt panic, slightly, in the back of his car. Occasionally, Emma would turn to talk to me but not enough to make me feel welcome. It seemed that her real conversation was with Enrique in Spanish and every so often she would throw me a charitable bone, as if remembering suddenly that she should be polite to her visitor. I felt discomfort rather than loneliness at first, that would come later. At traffic lights small children, some really tiny, would leap out of the shadows and start wiping the windscreen hoping to be paid. I never got used to this spectacle however often I witnessed it in the subsequent months. I was always convinced one of them would be run over when the traffic lights turned green.

Everything felt grubby and overwhelming, my own clothes were stinking of sweat and sticking to me. When we arrived at Emma's apartment building, which was low and squat with metal stairs on the outside, Emma and Enrique came up with me. She unlocked the door with several keys, it seemed excessively secure, and we all stood inside the room. There was an abundance of windows, all at waist height. There was a view of the highway lights, blurred like squashed stars and the traffic roared. The city was melting into the night. Emma showed me the bathroom. It was extremely basic. It had one of those showers that was positioned almost directly over the toilet so that everything was wet all the time. We all stood there and then Emma turned to me;

"Alright then, see you in the morning."

The two of them left me. I guess she was going to Enrique's. I was shocked to be stranded on my own so abruptly. I took my shoes of and dumped my backpack onto the floor. I sat on the unmade mattress. It smelly musty. The light outside was a violent pink and I wanted to cry but I stopped myself. My stomach squirmed with hunger. I went towards the makeshift 'kitchen' area.

There was a miniscule portable stove and a camping fridge. An ugly brown cupboard took up most of the space. I opened it and jolted backwards quickly in shock. It was teeming with ants. Inside were some American foodstuffs which I had never heard of, biscuits and crisps. I shook the packets and then ate standing there, shovelling them into my mouth, depositing crumbs on the dirty wooden floor. Almost immediately I felt an extreme dryness scrape against my throat. In the fridge was one solitary bottle of coke. A small glass bottle and I felt a brief flash of pure joy before I realised that there was no opener anywhere. There were limited places to look, but I searched doggedly. Apart from the monstrous brown cupboard in the kitchen, there was an old-fashioned, rather ornate chest of drawers and several suitcases lying messily open, giving the impression of transience. I searched everywhere for the bottle opener in a desperate hopeless way. I rifled through underwear in the chest of drawers and through socks and unnecessary heavy sweaters. In the lining of the suitcase, I found bundles of cash and I stared at them. They were tidy little rolls like a bank robber may have, I gazed upon them for a while transfixed but then put them back exactly where they were.

I felt frenzied then. I thought I may actually smash the bottle. Then I remembered that I was alone, more alone than I had ever been. If I had some kind of glass related accident no one would appear to save me. I drank water, in the end, from the tap and hoped for the best.

When it got completely dark, I didn't put the lights on because there were no curtains. I stripped off my clothes and had a tepid shower under a tiny trickle of water which managed to splash and soak everything nonetheless. I put on a t-shirt and pants and got into bed which smelt even more rancid close up and of other people. I cried then.

I wouldn't have thought it possible after having cried myself to sleep, but I was so exhausted that I slept solidly and in the harsh morning woke sweating with the sunlight glaring. I felt a glimmer of optimistic excitement. In all my searching the previous night I had unearthed a couple of keys which looked as if they may be spare keys to this flat. I dressed quickly, crouching under the wide windows, shoved some cash and the keys into the pockets of my jeans and left, locking the door carefully behind me.

The heat hit me again like a thick blanket. I started walking along the side of the highway, on the narrow sidewalk. Emma had told me that she lived on the edge of Coyoacan, the pretty, trendy area, so I headed there. The air stank. It was no doubt the humidity combined with the pollution and it felt hard to breathe, as if there was not enough space in my lungs. Later, I learnt that people often struggled to adjust to the altitude of Mexico City, but I didn't know that then. I worried that there was something wrong with me. Coyoacan was only ten minutes away but it was not a comfortable walk and my optimism was abating.

Monstrous American cars clogged up the highway, Men beeped their horns and shouted out at me, their voices blurring in the traffic. It sounded guttural and cajoling:

"Mamacita! Mamacita!"

I kept my head down. There were cars I recognised from films; Cadillacs and pickup trucks as well as ruined desperate machines which should never have been on the road and the taxis were green VW beetles. I used to think that they were cute. There were so many of them, like an invasion, every second car was a green beetle with a distinctive white roof.

Coyoacan was a calming oasis after the fury of the highway. It was exactly how I had imagined Mexico to be. There were cobbled streets, Baroque, colonial, brightly painted houses, gregarious street vendors and colourful artisan markets. Upscale cafes lined the cobbles and I wandered into one and ordered a coffee in bad Spanish. I sat in peaceful triumph. Finally, I thought, this was exactly the sort of experience that I was seeking. I watched the tourists milling about and the brisk Mexicans, dressed for business. School children passed, chattering in uniform, I was sitting partway behind a massive cactus and felt happily invisible. The waiter returned with quite a strange looking coffee. Perhaps this is what coffee looks like in Mexico, I mused. It tasted of spices and cinnamon, rich and exotic. He brought me the bill and I blanched. I barely had enough in my pocket to cover it. Afterwards, conscious that I had no cash left, I wandered around aimlessly. It got busier. Tourists arrived on tour buses in droves and huddled about in huge groups taking up the sidewalk. I started to feel the churning emptiness in my stomach and headed back to Emma's flat.

I was just fiddling with the key when she flung the door open wide from the inside.

"Where were you?" she cried, looking irate, "I was worried." She looked cross though, not concerned.

"Oh, I just went for a walk." I hated myself for sounding apologetic. After all, there was nothing to apologise for.

She was alone, no sign of Enrique, and snappily dressed again. She wore jeans and a sleeveless black vest. She looked extremely toned as if she had been working out.

"I thought that we could hang out. There's a cool place called Xochimilco."

"Sure!" I mumbled, trying to ignore the hunger pangs in my stomach. She seemed to be in a hurry. I had never known this variant of Emma before; in charge and controlling, like an older person. I was perplexed, but also given the current situation, relieved. Of course, I had no idea where I was or what was going on. I shoved more cash into my pocket.

We took several metro trains and then an overground. I had pushed my hair back, I wore a baggy t-shirt, I tried to make myself as inconspicuous as possible but still men stared with greedy, probing eyes. Emma kept repeating 'Be careful, be careful' and on the underground we sat deliberately between some women but I felt the eyes of the men burning through me. For the first time in my life, I questioned why this had ever been anything which anyone cleaved to, this attention from men. Here it seemed stripped bare, shown for what it was, dangerous and grubby.

Before arriving at the canals of Xochimilco, we walked through an extremely poor neighbourhood. It looked nothing like Coyoacan, it was dirty and smelly. Some of the houses were still brightly painted but they had a downtrodden air about them. However, this was a well-worn tourist trail and once on board a barge, we drifted down with all the other visitors, the mariachi bands competing for attention and for tips. Emma sat in the barge with her eyes shut, as if she was bored. She had obviously done this many times before. Every so often she opened her eyes and smiled at me in a superficial kind of way. The driver kept up a constant stream of conversation in broken English, directed at me. I tried to keep up but he was difficult to understand. I wanted to be kind. I was still hungry and starting to feel light-headed. Another barge floated by selling food.

"Get a torta!" said Emma in her new bored voice, still with her eyes half-shut. I negotiated clumsily with the lady in the barge and probably paid well over the odds, but the money, in any case, didn't make much sense to me yet. The torta was delicious. I felt in that moment, because I was so ravenous, that it was actually the most amazing thing that I had ever eaten. Happiness visited me briefly.

Chapter 3

Emma spent that first week with me. Just days, never nights. She would pick me up from her flat in the morning and return me there at some point in the afternoon and then she went off to see Enrique. She told me she had taken a week off from her job at the language school to show me around. The way that she said it was kind of petulant as if I should be grateful. In general, her attitude as she dutifully 'showed me around' was slightly begrudging. I was an inconvenience, that was the impression that I got. She never talked to me about Enrique. She didn't want me physically near him, that was obvious but neither did she want him in my thoughts. When she did talk, it was often about the language school in which she worked, Elite College, her boss (whom nobody liked) and her colleagues, the other teachers. Apparently, they were mainly misfits from the states, 'Gringos' she said dismissively. I resisted pointing out that in the eyes of the Mexicans, we too were 'Gringos'.

During that week, we visited mainly attractions in the Centro Historico. We wandered languidly, with various degrees of interest around the Zocalo, the Plaza de la Constitucion, the National Palace, the Metropolitan Cathedral and the Templo Mayor with its Aztec Ruins. We visited every sight on the tourist map. We admired the murals by Diego Riviera at the Secretaria de Educacion Publica. For lunch we always had street food. Emma claimed that it was safe though I was a bit dubious. We had tacos, tamales, quesadillas, but tortas remained my absolute favourite.

I always dressed as scruffily as possible; baggy everything, no make-up, hair scraped back. I hated the constant male attention. It seemed disrespectful and intrusive and put me on edge. Emma seemed to have no such qualms. She had reinvented herself in Mexico. She wore vests and shorts and her hair swung glossily over her shoulders. She paraded through the streets as if oblivious to all the gawking, as if cutting through silk. Was it a snub to me in some way? I don't know. I felt lost and dependent on her. This city, huge and overwhelming and foreign, engulfed me. I was a fish out of water and she knew it. One afternoon, late, we were drowsy with the heat and the fumes, she leapt out of the metro before me and then the doors shut, trapping me on the train. I felt panic rise in me then. I stood with my back against the glass divider staring down at the grubby floor, my heart beat erratic. She was waiting at the next stop but I couldn't shake the feeling that she had done it deliberately, to teach me a lesson, to prove her power in that instance.

Towards the end of that first week, I got sick. It must have been the street food because at 'home' I just ate boxed crackers from the US. Fever came in the night and sweat drenched the already gritty sheets. In the morning, sunlight burnt through the multiple windows and I felt dazed in a drifting dream state. It wasn't entirely unpleasant. I spent a lot of time hogging the toilet with the shower depositing annoying drips onto my head. In between I slept, a deep giddy sleep. Emma came in once. There was no phone in the room, no way for me to get in touch with her. She sniffed in a disgusted way and left. However, the next day she returned with an older man, whom she introduced as the father of Enrique, a doctor.

 They both stood by the dishevelled stinking mattress looking at me. Enrique's dad was tall, like his son, with the same gangling dark honey- coloured limbs and his face was kind. He gave me some medicine to take. The writing was in Spanish and I had no idea what it was, but I took it anyway. He told me to drink a lot of water and coke. Emma, to her credit, went to buy large bottles and left them next to the mattress. The coke felt lovely, sugary in my sour tasting mouth. After several days, which seemed to have bled together in a fog, I felt myself emerge, weakened but stable, like a new born animal on shaky legs.

We conducted a few more tentative outings. We went to the Frida Kahlo museum in Coyoacan. We saw an art exhibition at the Museo Universitario Arte Contemporaneo. I could never shake the impression that Emma was just showing me around out of duty. Sometimes, she would mitigate this impression by, strangely, confiding in me. One day we were sitting in a park, on a bench, drinking cold bottles of coke. I treated coke like medicine then, somehow believing that it was the wonder drug which had cured my stomach. I would drink one a day. Anyway, apropos to nothing, she told me that Enrique had a deep sadness within him. It was a strange turn of phrase and I stared at her, I could feel that my eyebrows were raised. "Oh, why is that?" I asked, touched and surprised that she wanted to talk to me about anything personal.

"He had a twin sister who died when he was a baby."

Emma was wearing sunglasses and she looked out at the straggly greenery before us, assuming, I thought meanly, a tragic pose, her chin uplifted.

"That's sad." I said in a mournful voice. "How did she die?"

"Oh, I can't tell you that!" She looked at me aghast, "That would be betraying a confidence!"

Why bother telling me anything, I thought, suddenly furious. She stood up abruptly and then turned to me pensively once more. I couldn't see her eyes because of the sunglasses and the shadows cast by the great tress behind us;

"Sometimes I think he sees me as a long-lost sister rather than as a girlfriend."

She didn't talk to me for a while after that. It was as if she had betrayed herself, her insecurities in a moment of weakness. In any case, it was never to be repeated.

We never ate street food again together, because of my stomach. We went to restaurants and for a few days I stuck to soup. I had the impression that Emma blamed me for this too. It took a while to get my strength back, I still felt wobbly. Emma called me a 'gringo' because 'gringos' could never handle the food. I kept my mouth shut.

Barely ten days had passed since I had landed in Mexico, when Emma said gravely;

"We've got to talk."

She followed me into her flat. That was a rare occurrence in itself, she usually left me at the door. She told me that I couldn't stay there any longer. My immediate thought was that I should just go back home to the UK. Then, almost immediately, I imagined how stupid it would look that my gap year adventure had only lasted ten days.

I just kind of gaped at her. Where should I go? A youth hostel? I barely had any money, I hadn't planned to spend money on rent, not on my own. I was kind of expecting to stay with Emma and to contribute to her costs. I still found the sheer size and scale of DF intimidating without Emma by my side. I hated how vulnerable this made me, how dependant on her.

She studied the expression on my face and then explained how one of the gringos whom she worked with, Brad, was moving back to the States and that maybe I could have his room. In a placatory fashion, she added that maybe I could find a job in Elite as well as Brad would be leaving a vacancy. I jumped into this idea happily and by the next day I had the number of Brad's ex-landlady. I went out to find a payphone and after several botched attempts, I got through.

The lady was called Elena and spoke very basic English. She was friendly, obviously pleased that there would be no break in rental income. In fact, in the event, Brad moved out one day (I never met him) and I moved in the next. I left Emma's flat mid-morning, she didn't say goodbye, but Elena's flat did have a phone and she claimed that she would be in touch. I got a beetle cab with my backpack to my new address. I had been informed that it was in a reasonably safe neighbourhood in Del Valle, Narvarte.

Chapter 4

From what I gleaned during that cab journey, Narvarte is pretty close to Coyoacan so I finally felt a twinge of welcome familiarity. It was the first time that I had managed to get any bearings at all. It felt like a small triumph. Even getting a cab on my own had felt like an achievement.

My new abode was on the first floor of a low, unassuming block of apartments. However, once inside the entrance hall was ornate and lavish in that typical Mexican way that I was becoming accustomed to; deep russet- coloured walls with a turquoise border. The windows were shuttered with elaborately patterned wooden blinds. A sweeping staircase led to the first floor. Elena's compact apartment was in keeping with the theme, but there the walls were painted a sunny yellow. The front door opened directly onto the living room which was like a show case to Mexican interior design and, I was soon to learn, was lived in by no one, not Elena and not myself. It looked too grand. 'My' room was a large double and Elena had her own similarly sized room down the hall. It was stuffed to the brim full of knick knacks as if to keep the living room as a museum piece. The bathroom and kitchen were unremarkable. The kitchen was miniscule and overrun by ants. It seemed to be a recurrent issue in DF.

Elena herself was efficient and smart. She worked in an office in the business district. Even on her days off, as I was soon to discover, she dressed as if she were heading to work. She was never without her heels. The minute she left her bedroom, she put them on. During the entire time that I lived there, I saw her rarely but when she did see me, she went out of her way to be pleasant. Sometimes even exceptionally warm.

More than a week had passed since I had left Emma and moved to Narvarte and I still hadn't heard from her. I had no way of contacting her. She knew where I was and she knew my new number but she didn't call. As the days passed, I staunchly adhered to my role as independent adventurer but inside I felt a sinking abandonment. I spent my time going on long lonely walks around my new neighbourhood. It was a random mix of residential and retail encircled by the ubiquitous roaring highways with their haze of toxic pollution.

There was a lovely rustic restaurant opposite the flat which would make me tortas whenever I wanted. I used to sit at one of their wooden tables, unadorned, often the place would be empty. The owners, I presumed, an older couple, would make me the torta and then silently watch me eat it, their faces round and serious. I also grew to love tamales, the spicier the better, washed down with cups of fresh orange juice. My episode of food poisoning felt like a distant memory now and I grew braver. The food you could buy on the street or in small restaurants was so cheap that I never bothered to cook. I had never had any inclination to do so anyway. I no longer worried about getting sick, I figured, somewhat irrationally, that I was hardier now. I would also buy American cereals from the supermarket. Often men would follow me, up and down the aisles of the shop or, worse, on the street. I wore trainers. If they persisted, I ran. The American cereals were brightly coloured and sugary and hurt my teeth. Elena, when she saw them, laughed and mumbled something in Spanish. I didn't understand but presumed it was along the lines of 'fucking gringo'.

One day, I walked the long grim route by the side of the highway, depressingly accustomed now to the fumes, to get to the library. It was an old round building situated in the middle of a pretty park. It was a rigmarole to join but finally I worked it out and left with some Charles Dickens books, which were the only English language books that they had. I sat on my bed smoking and reading with the window open. Mexican voices flowed up from the street. Soon, I discovered that a tiny shop just across the way, barely visible from the street, sold cheap Mexican beer. So, I added that to my routine.

One afternoon, I gave Elena some cash and phoned my parents. My dad answered and sounded overjoyed to hear from me. He asked if I was having fun with Emma. I felt like crying then, my voice got thick with tears, but I didn't have the heart to tell him that Emma had basically ditched me. I told him, truthfully, about the places we'd seen and the new and exotic food that I'd eaten. He was always, still, interested in hearing about 'fancy' food as he called it, it amused him. I gave him all the details, omitting to mention that the street food had made me sick. I could almost hear him grinning and licking his lips when I told him what ingredients they put in tortas. My dad was a hypothetical foodie. My mum was out somewhere. Recently, she had been going out more often. I just thought that she was more sociable than my dad, less home oriented. I looked out of the window at the harsh Mexican sun and pictured her scurrying about in all her finery in our bleak, rainy town. I felt a sharp pain in my stomach when we said goodbye and had to remain sitting where I was, leaning against the vivid yellow wall, my bare feet cool on the floor tiles.

That evening I ate some sugary cereal and went to bed early, listlessly. I lay in bed smoking and drinking beer as usual. In the vague distant background was the roar of the omnipresent highway with its leering drivers. The ex-tenant, Brad, had left a fluffy blue hoodie in one of the cupboards. It smelt of aftershave and when I felt really lonely, I put it on. How sad, I thought, to crave connection with some unknown gringo, some misfit. Some loser.

Fortunately, Emma called the next morning because things were starting to feel very unhappy for me.

"Hey!" she cried in an artificial sing song voice as if we'd been chatting every day.

"I told Stefan at Elite about you!" I remembered that Stefan was the boss who nobody liked. "He really wants to meet you, can you come in today?"

She started giving me instructions for the metro but then seemed to recall how hopeless I was, sighed and gave up.

"Just jump into a cab, it's not very far."

It was pretty far and the traffic fumes had their usual soporific effect on me so that by the time I arrived, I felt dopey and dazed. Emma was waiting outside an ugly office block for me looking smart and carrying a book bag. The only evidence that there was a language school inside the building was a tiny sticker saying 'Elite' next to the buzzer. Not even 'language school', it could have been an escort agency.

We walked up four flights of stairs. There was no lift. The stairs were concrete and worn and the strip lighting overhead spoke of depressing office blocks everywhere. Elite language school occupied one floor and the reception area was surprisingly professional. It far exceeded my expectations. A bespectacled, older Mexican lady manned the front desk. I was later to find out that she and her husband owned the school. Stefan was the Director of Studies and basically ran it on a day-to-day basis and was responsible for the hiring. The lady beamed at Emma and stared at me. She said something in rapid Spanish and Emma nodded in agreement but also rolled her eyes. As we moved down the hall, I asked Emma what she'd said.

"Oh, she said that you were very beautiful." replied Emma in a bored voice, managing to convey by her tone that she couldn't believe that shit was still going on.

Stefan looked like an annoying person and he was. A reedy tall man with an orange wispy beard, he obviously thought a great deal of himself. He spoke in a clipped, formal English. His first language was German but his English grammar was better than mine, I could tell that straight away. He kept repeating "Yah Yah" like some demented Sloane ranger and I wondered where he had picked that up. He didn't stare at me, he barely looked at me. I was just a shape to be talked at. Emma later told me that everyone thought that he was gay, so that explained the lack of staring. He hired me straightaway. They needed a native English speaker.

"But what about the teaching part?" I asked Emma in a panic.

"Oh, don't worry, you just follow a book." she waved her hand dismissively.

I was shown to the staffroom, which looked a lot like a compact version of our secondary school library. Tatty, dog-eared textbooks and dictionaries lined the shelves along with loose piles of paper in boxes, seemingly random. There was a basic, squat computer.

"Nobody uses it, it's broken." Emma told me.

Also, a photocopier.

"You're only allowed to make five copies a day, it's such a pain in the arse." Emma complained mysteriously. I had no idea what she meant at the time, it was only when I had to teach a class of twenty and only two of them had books that I realised why that was so painfully relevant.

I was to be teaching the Elementary class every morning from 9-12. Everyone in my class was supposed to have bought the text book which we would be using from the school, at obviously greatly inflated prices. I looked at the text book. There was a reading, a listening, some grammar exercises, and some phonetic stuff which I didn't understand.

"Where are the answers?" I asked, turning to the back of the book and not locating them.

"There should be a teacher's book, but most of them have gone missing. Anyway, it's elementary, you'll be fine." I could tell that she was losing interest in me and in the conversation.

The teachers who had been in class started to trickle back into the staffroom. There was a hippyish, chubby blonde girl who looked friendly and dippy and two young men. All gringos, I presumed. A skinny dark one with sideburns looked me up and down with a familiar leer.

"Is this Brad's replacement then? I'll take her over that asshole any day!"

The other boy snorted and, without acknowledging me at all, headed towards the shelves.

"Eduardo is pissing me off today." he announced to the room. Noone replied.

"My name is Penny." the blonde girl smiled valiantly at me, obviously trying to make up for the other two.

"Pleased to meet you." I sounded posh and British, even to my own ears and I saw the men exchange glances.

A loud thought came into my head then: I want to go home. But I knew that it wasn't an option. That would be failing.

That day was Friday and I was to start work on Monday. The whole thing seemed so ludicrous that I couldn't believe that it was actually real but I was handed a document which was a contract of some kind and it had an immediate sobering effect on me. A tiny part of me was the optimistic cheerleader but most of me was just pure panic. I had never stood in front of a group of people before, not since school plays in primary school. I didn't know anything about grammar. All weekend, I stared at 'Unit 1' of my class text book trying to work it out. Painstakingly, I did all the exercises myself; the reading, the prepositions, the greetings which involved something called 'intonation' but I didn't know what that meant so I decided to skip it. I should have brought a dictionary home with me. There was a listening too, but apparently the tapes were kept in the classroom so I thought I'd cross that bridge when I came to it.

Chapter 5

On Sunday night I couldn't sleep. I had a beer and read 'A Tale of two Cities' but it was quite hard going and I couldn't really concentrate. I was very nervous about the following day. I thought I'd try to put my head down at around ten, so that's when I turned the lights out and closed my eyes. I listened to the distant screech and roar of the highway and the tinny voices coming from the TV in Elena's room. I tried to think pleasant thoughts, imagine happy scenarios but I couldn't think of any happy scenarios which were even borderline realistic. My imagination didn't deal with pure fantasy. I pictured myself at university the following year, surrounded by friends and popular. I struggled to picture it because I realised, suddenly, in that instant (my eyes pinged open), that I had never been popular and that tragically, Emma was the closest thing to a friend that I had.

I wondered why.

Maybe I was just intrinsically bad. It couldn't just be because I was too good-looking. I sat up and lit a cigarette, fumbling about on the nightstand for the cheap plastic lighter, one of many which I kept losing. There was something about the tip of the cigarette waving about in the gloom, me sitting there with the heavy glass ashtray on my lap on top of the sheets, the colourful Mexican blanket kicked off and bunched on the floor. There was something about all of that which made tears trickle down my cheeks. I went to pee and when I got back into bed my mouth tasted foul because of the cigarette so I got up again to brush my teeth. It was midnight by then, so said my small digital clock. I turned it the other way so that I didn't have to look at it. I thought about how things may improve if I was working and making friends and then I thought about the men in the staffroom and I turned the clock around again and it said 1:22. I thought about how I would change my image when I went to university. I would dress down, in baggy clothes, no make-up, like I did here. I could reinvent myself. I could join new clubs and societies, explore novel pastimes. I wasn't sporty but maybe something like chess? I pictured myself with a motley collection of geeks, wearing glasses in a big-domed library, sitting around a chessboard, studious and intense. I had another cigarette. My heart was beating fast. I couldn't be bothered to brush my teeth, I felt weakened, so I squirted some toothpaste into my mouth and chewed it. The flat felt empty, even though I knew Elena was there. Outside a dog howled, there were still traffic noises. I was almost relieved. I felt slightly less cast adrift. It was 3:46 by then and I just gave up. I lay on my back with my eyes open staring at the almost pitch blackness. I must have drifted off because when the alarm went off at 7am, it felt like I was being dragged up from the bottom of the sea. My eyes were gritty and toothpaste was crusted drily at the corners of my lips.

I had a shower and a coffee which was too strong and swished about my empty stomach and made me shaky.

By 9 am I was standing in front of my Elementary class of eight students. Emma, who I had seen briefly as she sashayed in and out of the classroom, told me that Mondays were always slow. I noticed that three of my students had books. There were five females and three males. Out of the ladies, two were much older, late middle-age, and one of the men was older, in a business suit. The other two were roughly my age. All of them stared at me with serious faces and then turned to each other and started chatting, obviously about me. One of the girls started laughing with her mouth open. My heart was hammering in my ears.

"Hello class!" I boomed in my loudest voice, it sounded like a shout to my ears.

"Hello teacher!" shouted back the man in the business suit and then looked around the class with hilarity on his face. I decided that he was going to be a pain in the arse.

"My name is Abby!" I looked around for a pen with which to write on the whiteboard but it was running out and my name could barely be seen, a faded grey smear.

"My name is Javier!" shouted suit man.

I ignored him and tried to catch the eyes of the other students.

"What are your names?" I lowered my voice slightly. They told me but I instantly forgot.

"Today," I waved my book at them, "We are going to be studying unit 1."

They looked at each other perplexed and some rapid chatting took place.

"Teacher! Teacher!" shouted Javier

"Abby, please!"

"Teacher Abby! We do Unit 4."

"No, Unit 1, page 7"

"No!" shouted Javier, increasingly irate, "Unit 1,2,3 finish! FINISH! Now Unit 4!"

At last, I understood. My heart sank. I realised then how stupid I had been. Of course, it wouldn't be Unit 1, it was halfway through a term. I forced myself to turn calmly to unit 4 but inside I was frantic. I was only familiar with Unit 1. The sleepless night added to the sense of panic and vague nausea. Unit 4 followed the same format. I could see that. The grammar consisted of the present perfect. Unfortunately, I had no idea what that was. The students huddled round the three books and took it in turns to read the text. It was slow going and two of the younger girls chatted constantly. It was only 9:20, break wasn't until 10:30, it all seemed painfully interminable. They took it in turns to answer the questions and then, fortuitously, I found the ancient tape recorder and, somewhat triumphantly, the corresponding tape. We listened to the tape three times, by which time I felt confident that I knew the answers.

At break, I felt great relief. I thought I may be able to pull it off. I was tentatively optimistic.

Penny smiled at me and I felt, in that second, a glimmer of happiness.

"So how is it going?"

"Fine, I think we've almost finished Unit 4"

One of the gringos who was there, but who had thus far completely ignored me, snorted.

"Oh honey!" said Penny mournfully and my spirits sank.

"What?"

"You know each unit has to last a week, right?" She spoke slowly as if talking to a child.

"But how?" I felt quite desperate, exhausted and hopeless.

"How can I make it last longer?"

The darker gringo turned to me with barely suppressed venom.

"Seriously? Where the fuck did they find you? It's not about being pretty in here you know!"

"Ed! Shut up!" hissed Penny

She pointed to the chaotic shelves.

"You pad it out with lots of games and activities…Look, they are split according to level. Elementary are right here."

She gestured for me to get closer to her.

I leaned in and she whispered.

"We're only supposed to make five copies a day but wait until these assholes two piss off and you can make as many as you like." She gave me a conspiratorial wink.

I worked it out then. It was a steep learning curve and the first week was very shaky with a lot of last minute 'padding' activities. Penny explained to me what the present perfect was, and then how it differed from the past simple. I expected scathing remarks from the gringos and I wasn't disappointed. I grew accustomed to ignoring them. However, Emma wasn't exactly supportive either. She came into the staffroom during one of Penny's grammar explanations and exclaimed,

"Seriously, how do you not know that stuff?"

Teaching gave a structure to the day though, which was helpful for my state of mind. After work, I got the metro home, usually got myself a torta to take away from the restaurant opposite and sat on my bed eating it. After I had a cigarette, a read and a long nap. I woke up late afternoon. I would have a coffee and start prepping for the next day. I was diligent because I had nothing else to do. It was a solitary existence, made bearable by Penny, who was kind with no caveat. Just purely kind. One day she asked if I wanted to have lunch after class and then that became our routine.

 Close to the school was an outdoor food market which I had never seen before. It was lively and colourful and packed with students. Sitting there with Penny, trying different foods, I felt briefly content, as if I was living the genuine gap year experience. Genuinely enjoying the exotic and strange as I should be, albeit in culinary form.

After a while, Penny explained that she had escaped an abusive husband in California. I stared at her. She was much older than I had originally thought, twenty-nine. Her round, smooth face was deceptively youthful. After a few weeks of our lunches together, her story came out in drips and drabs and then in chunks.

 She told me that she had gone to a very sporty high school in her home town in California and she had not been popular there at all. She had struggled to make any friends. She herself was not involved in sport or cheerleading or anything of that nature. She enjoyed music, actually, playing the piano, but that was considered square. She didn't want to complain to her parents as the school had an excellent reputation and she didn't want to seem ungrateful and let them down. It did seem, however, that every single person was either running or throwing a ball or doing back flips and she could do none of those things so she felt like a weirdo. Really, she felt so miserable that she even started harming herself. Not because it was fashionable or because the cool kids were doing it, but because she realised that if she cut her skin somewhere on her legs or her arms, somewhere hidden, then it would feel like a release and some of the intense loneliness and frustration that she felt would drain away. This went on for some time and her parents never noticed. To their credit, she kept the evidence of the self-harm very well concealed, she always wore long sleeves and jeans, even when it was baking outside. That should have been a clue, she laughed quite bitterly then, they were in California, after all, and she was wearing such inappropriate clothing. It was fucking hot! She lit a cigarette, inhaled deeply, and went on.

One day she was standing by her locker looking for something, when she was surprised by one of the cooler boys, Jesse, who played football. She didn't follow football, of course, but she knew that he was considered something of a hot shot. In any case, he had never so much as looked at her before and that day, there he was, standing right in front of her. He was very handsome. She had noticed that before, in the kind of detached way that you notice that actors are handsome. Lovely, but nothing to do with you. He was smiling at her and instinctively she looked behind her just in case she was mistaken and he was actually smiling instead at one of his cool gang.

But, no, he was smiling at her!

He asked her politely to go to a dance with him. She had known, vaguely, that there was a dance coming up. There were always dances to which the cool kids went and she had never got involved up until then. She just stared at him. She couldn't believe that this scenario was actually taking place. It seemed surreal. Surely, she would have noticed if he had shown any interest in her before? If he had been looking at her even? How was she possibly his type anyway? His whole gang were slim and beautiful and she was…she looked at Abby then with a mock despairing look…well plump, just like now. I have always been this size! She shrugged. It doesn't bother me now, she told me, but it did then! Anyway, after gaping like a fish at Jesse for a while, she did eventually say yes and he took her to the dance.

On that night, and also on all the subsequent nights that they spent together, he kept her away from the rest of his sporty gang and he was actually very sweet to her. He was much more down to earth and kind than she had thought he would be. The rest of his gang were flashy and wealthy, but actually, his family were from a similar social demographic to hers. He was that great at football, that he had sports sponsors, a concept that even now, years later, she didn't fully comprehend…anyway, in practical terms, it meant that he was actually paid to play football and hence could afford the fancy car and designer clothes which allowed him to fit in. Unlike Penny.

Jesse and Penny became a couple. It was great, Penny told me, lighting another cigarette, as long as they kept away from the rest of his friends. He had this lovely little sister and his mum and dad were super young and really relaxed. They had the best time just hanging around his house playing cards with his family. Unfortunately, Jesse didn't often want to do that. He wanted to be out with his friends showing off in his fancy car. He even realised, he had told Penny, how immature that was, but as a disclaimer he had chuckled and added, 'We are young after all, aren't we? We need to have fun!'

It wasn't fun, not for Penny though, not at all. As soon as Jesse's back was turned, the cool gang ignored her at best, sometimes they were downright mean. One of his supposed best friends, a massive muscley boy called Wayne told her once that Jesse had only asked her out originally as a dare, and he Wayne, was amazed that the relationship had lasted, that she, Penny, was definitely not his type and incongruous to his lifestyle.

"He actually said that! 'Incongruous to his lifestyle', I'll never forget it!" Penny inhaled deeply. We both looked around at the sweltering polluted Mexican street. I had been so involved in the story, that I had forgotten where we were. It felt a bit like coming out of a cinema into the harsh daylight.

"Anyway," continued Penny, "Wayne was the worst of the bunch, really toxic."

We ordered another juice and I told her to go on. Every time that they had all gone out together, Wayne would find an opportunity to tell her that Jesse was too good for her or words to that effect. She didn't know what his fucking problem was! He, himself was surrounded by stunning women and was also some kind of high-level jock. Penny had no idea what his issue was with her, but it reached a head a few years later, just after they all graduated high school. They were eighteen. Penny discovered, shortly after their graduation ceremony, that she was pregnant.

It was a shock. It was a small town and like all small towns, conservative. Everyone, both sets of parents, expected them to get married. Weirdly, thinking about it now, she had never considered having an abortion. Probably because she would have had no idea how to go about it, where even to go. Everyone in town knew her! Both her and Jesse were fundamentally clueless about everything. It was no one's fault, ultimately, what happened.

"What did happen?" I asked

"Well, I lost the baby right after the marriage ceremony…about two days after. My parents had paid for it. It wasn't super fancy or anything, but it was done properly, you know. In a community like that, you had to do things properly. Basically, in the same way as everyone else…all fucking Stepford sheep!" she laughed bitterly.

"So," she went on," of course, it felt like there had been no point to the marriage now that there wasn't even a baby! But there we were stuck with each other. There was resentment brewing on both sides. We didn't want to be married. The implication was that we now get jobs, neither of us had excelled at school or anything, so our options were really limited. We had this tiny flat. The air conditioning never worked and it was always really humid and damp and Wayne was always there, rolling joints, and the smell would just linger and linger until I felt as if I was literally stoned all the time. He still hated me…now more than ever…he felt as if I had trapped Jesse. He even insinuated that maybe I had made up the pregnancy to start with! Such an asshole!"

"Maybe," Penny turned to me laughing, "And, this has just occurred to me…maybe Wayne wanted Jesse for himself, you know, as more than just a friend!"

"Anyway, Jesse wasn't quite talented enough to be a professional sportsman, which was another blow of course and knocked his confidence. Instead, he coached high school football, in the school which he had just graduated from! He didn't enjoy it though. It made him feel like a failure. Every time he went in there to work, he was reminded how fantastic things had been expected of him and had ultimately, failed to materialise and then things got even worse…"

"What happened then?" I asked, a bit too eagerly

"I'm kind of exhausted now," Penny sighed "and this story just gets sadder."

It was true that we had been sitting in the same street café for hours and the owner was giving us funny looks. Penny's voice had become increasingly hoarse with all the nervous cigarettes and the pollution. We decided to leave the next instalment for another day.

The following day, I couldn't wait for lunchtime to hear the rest of Penny's tale. I don't know why it was so enthralling for me, probably because it provided a distraction from my own unhappiness and extreme loneliness. I would picture California, to which I had never been, to be a bit like Mexico, hot and polluted and dusty with massive highways.

"Not so much pollution, no," laughed Penny, "Not nearly as much, and all the restaurants are these depressing cheesy plastic buildings, and they are all the same everywhere, no originality, no character…just huge plates of beige stodge served to huge beige people."

Penny was vegetarian, and American food was a particular bugbear for her, but I didn't want her to start going on about that now, I wanted her to carry on with her story.

"With Jesse, something happened then, at work?" I prompted.

"No," she went on," not at work ironically. There he was coaching every day, and then one Saturday, he goes for a run in the park and he tripped on a branch and fell awkwardly. It was just massively unlucky. He broke his ankle in such a complicated way that it refused to mend properly and he was in terrible pain. All the time. In this dreadful mood, of course, logically enough, and in the most dreadful pain. Hobbling round on his crutches and shouting at me all day, it was awful. I forgot to tell you", she added," I had a job as a secretary in a little accountancy firm at the time. It was really boring, but when Jesse got nasty, I was happy to escape there. At least it was somewhere that I could legitimately go. My parent's attitude at the time was that I had made my bed, literally, and now I had to lie in it. Kind of harsh, now I think about it…anyway…the doctor gave Jesse a super strong painkiller. It was common at the time, about half the town was taking it for something.

It dealt with his pain, alright, the only problem was that it was an opiate, and Jesse, along with half the town, became addicted. He became extremely nasty when he didn't have it, and by nasty, I mean violent. He would attack me for any reason, no excuse too small. And then, she gulped, lit a cigarette, and then, even worse; some health body high up realised that all these Americans were getting addicted to these particular painkillers and withdrew them, basically overnight! I remember, the day that Jesse realised that he couldn't get hold of any more, he had rung everyone, all the doctors, all the pharmacies, it wasn't their fault, they just weren't allowed…he just roared at me, like an animal, this really deep primal roar and I just ran out of the house to my parents.

I couldn't tell them what was going on, not really, I felt embarrassed or ashamed, I don't know. I felt as if I had fucked up my life already, that it was all too late…anyway the next day, I came back…and…and…Wayne was there and there was this weird shit all over the living room floor and the coffee table and I had never seen it up close before, but I knew what it was, of course, all the weird fucking shit, it was heroin.

For ages I blamed Wayne. He was always there, like the devil, encouraging bad shit to take place, but really it was inevitable…all the people who had been addicted to the legitimate opiate then moved onto heroin and our lives, my life, became impossible and I left him and the town and my parents were mortified. They thought I should have been a good wife and stayed, that was the mentality then, but he didn't love me, he hated me by then, I am pretty sure…"

She grew quiet, and though it was not usual for us, I ordered a couple of beers. The waiter looked surprised, we always ordered juices only, but brought the beers happily with a grin and a flourish. We sat there, peacefully, staring at the humdrum street. I was shocked at all that she had been through. I had misjudged her based on her appearance, the way that people always misjudged me, I thought bitterly.

She was much more perceptive and intelligent than I had given her credit for previously, too. The hippyish appearance was extremely misleading. She had been in Mexico for years and working at Elite for years too. DF was not an easy place to live, especially as a lone gringo woman, she was clearly tough. She had moved around the city quite a bit, but was presently living with a couple of female Mexican students. She had little time for men. It was hardly surprising after the experience she'd had. Also, she couldn't stand our colleagues.

"Those fucking assholes we work with!" and then; "That fucking Brad was the worst."

Seriously, I almost felt betrayed. I had thought that the blue fluffy sweatshirt was my friend, now it felt contaminated. She told me Emma was pleasant but distant. I think that she was more pleasant to Penny than to me. With me, she was just distant. She greeted me when she saw me in the staffroom and sometimes asked me how my class was going, but that was it. It was as if she had done her duty by finding me a job and now, she could wash her hands of me. I felt a deep visceral hurt.

Months went by like this. I became friendly with certain members of my class too, the young girls. They had a sense of humour and there was ongoing banter, however I realised that I was always 'the teacher' and that they were never totally relaxed with me. It wasn't a natural friendship. Javier was always a pain in the arse but I became more and more confident and learnt to ignore him. I studied grammar in the afternoons and became very adept at utilising the resources in the staffroom and even at inventing my own games for the students. In short, I was pretty proud of myself. I had found something that I was proficient at.

Christmas, nevertheless, was obviously quite a sad time for me. I had always loved the lead up, all the school fairs and parties and secret Santas at home. Here, each of us had a little party in our classroom which basically involved eating Mexican cakes and biscuits. My students gave me a hug, although I ducked away from Javier. Then the school shut and I was alone. I had no idea where Emma was, she never told me. Penny was invited to stay with the family of one of her flatmates, in Puebla. Elena travelled to spend a few days with her aged parents in a village outside Mexico City. I watched the colourful Las Posadas in the centre, but I was very much the detached onlooker. The flat felt creepy without Elena in it and I kept all the lights on in the living room, the hall, the kitchen, overnight. I'd sit there in bed smoking, listening to revellers shouting and laughing outside.

On Christmas day, my parents phoned and I spoke to everyone, even my brother. My gran, my dad's mum was coming down from Leeds as she did every year, it was the tradition. We rarely saw her from one Christmas to the next. That year, I felt the sharp sour pain of nostalgia for the first time. I missed them all dreadfully. My dad and mum claimed that they missed me too, and they probably did, especially my dad, but they had other stuff going on, all the traditions to get through. My dad sounded a bit subdued on the phone, which wasn't like him. I asked him what was wrong but he couldn't tell me. Probably because he was surrounded by people. My mum told me that they had posted a present, but of course I hadn't received it yet. Mexican post was notoriously unreliable. It was more than likely that someone would steal whatever it was before I received it in any case.

Chapter 6

Then it all went wrong. Not suddenly, but gradually and then shockingly.

Emma came up to me in the staffroom one day. She sat down next to me and looked right at me as if she wanted to have a conversation. She was looking as glamourous as ever; her hair slick, her make up perfect. I was surprised that she wanted to talk to me, to say the least, but smiled amiably.

"Zoe is coming over for a couple of weeks." She told me, "I thought that we could show her around."

I was pathetically grateful to be included. I should have told her no, then and there. I should have had some pride but unfortunately, I still believed that they were my friends. I also felt kind of sorry for Zoe. I knew that she was spending her gap year working in a cheap supermarket, that she needed to pay for university herself. She couldn't afford to spend months away. This would probably be her only trip, her only normal student-like experience.

Emma took a couple of weeks off work for Zoe. It turned out that it was really easy to take time off work, not nearly the sacrifice that Emma had made out previously. Elite simply blended the classes together. They had to pay for one less teacher so the school really didn't care. It was true that there was no such thing as holiday pay, Emma hadn't lied about that.

Zoe arrived on the Monday. I didn't see neither her nor Emma all week and then on Thursday evening Emma called me at home. I had presumed, by then, that Emma had forgotten about including me and was surprised when the phone rang.

"Hi!" she was super friendly. I sat on the cold tiled floor and lit a cigarette.

"I was wondering if you wanted to come out with us on Friday night? We're going to check out this new club, Enrique knows the DJ."

I was so astonished that I was momentarily mute.

"Hello?" she rasped impatiently.

"Um, yes OK."

"Great! Things start late here so we'll swing by and pick you up around ten."

I was so bewildered by this turn of events that I stayed up late smoking and knocking back the cheap beer. Why would they want me to come along? Maybe Zoe had decided that she wanted to see me. Maybe Emma had had a change of heart and now thought that it would be the kind thing to do, to hang out with me. Did I want a pity invitation though? If that was what it was.

I was tired and befuddled the next morning at school and worried about staying awake until ten to go out. I was usually in bed by then, with my book and my beers. My parent's parcel, surprisingly, had arrived in early January and it contained a huge bundle of the latest paperbacks from the UK. It was such a great gift. I was getting really bored of Charles Dickens. In all honesty, I didn't want to go to a club, I wanted to stay in bed and read. I wish I had done.

Javier shouted at me;

"Teacher Abby! You sleepy!"

I ignored him as usual. He looked round the class to get a reaction and the other students ignored him too. I was getting better at teaching on auto-pilot. I didn't see Emma at all that day. She often got sent to companies to provide business English classes in-situ. Penny frowned at me in the break.

"Heavy night?"

"No, but actually I'm supposed to be going out tonight."

"Oh?"

"With Emma."

She looked puzzled, as well she might. She saw with what indifference Emma treated me.

That afternoon, I had a short superficial nap. I was anxious about that night and couldn't relax. If I had been completely honest with myself, I'd have refused the invitation, flattering though I thought it was. I wish I had. I really do. That night out ultimately destroyed everything.

I didn't get dressed up. I didn't even wear make-up. I scraped my hair back. All evening, I didn't know what to do with myself. I had a shower and sat there on my bed with a book and a packet of cigarettes, but I struggled to concentrate and the wait was interminable. They were late too. It was past 10.30 by the time that Emma pressed the buzzer and Elena come out of her room looking confused and a bit worried.

"Who is that?"

"My friend. I'm going out." Even I sounded incredulous.

"Out? Where at this time? Careful! Please be careful!" she sounded really worried then, as well as shocked.

I felt a grim sense of foreboding but brushed it off.

At the front door stood Emma and behind her I could see the sleek silhouette of Enrique's car, shiny and a bit ominous. Emma was really dressed up. She was wearing hot pants and knee-high boots and had glitter on her eyelids.

"What are you wearing?" she looked me up and down critically and sighed.

"Never mind, come on then."

I opened the back door to the car, expecting to see Zoe, and I did see Zoe, but sitting in the middle seat was Paul. Paul! Both Zoe and Paul turned to me with their identical moon faces but Paul's was wearing a massive grin and Zoe's was sporting make-up.

"Hi!" I mumbled, confused.

"I didn't realise that you were both here?"

"Yes, we are BOTH here." Zoe sighed. She didn't look too happy about it.

"Mum and dad wanted some time on their own…"

"Right." Even though I was right next to him in the car, Paul had his head turned like a wooden puppet, staring at me. Enrique grunted at me in greeting. I saw his beautiful eyes in the mirror, they blinked at me slowly, like the eyes of a feline, then looked away.

The car screeched off and entered the tumultuous roar of the endless highway. There was stilted chit chat in the back. Zoe and Paul had been given the standard DF tour and Paul had obviously found it far more exciting than Zoe, who was reserved with me to say the least. Whatever animosity Emma had towards me must have been catching. What did they have against me? Why was I even there? I wondered anew and then the reason slapped me in the face. Suddenly, it was so transparent! I was there for Paul. Of course. His little leering face was inches from mine. Paul was the one who had requested my presence.

We pulled up outside a club which looked like a club anywhere, we could have been anywhere in the world. A massive doorman and a row of pretty people. Enrique walked us straight to the front. I was still reeling from the fact that they had valet parking, something I'd only ever seen in films. We walked straight in. I hadn't realised that Enrique had that kind of influence. He looked impressive, the way that he took charge, attractive. He seemed older and somehow more powerful. Paul looked like a downtrodden puppy in comparison. Zoe was also dressed up but it didn't sit well on her. She was the wrong shape and she looked supremely uncomfortable in her mini-skirt and heels, her make-up garish in the pink lighting of the club, like a mask.

A waitress led us straight to the VIP area, which was on a slight platform with a view of the dancefloor and cordoned off with rope. As soon as we sat down, I noticed that people were staring at us. It was embarrassing. I felt conspicuous and ridiculous. Emma seemed to relish it though, lots of preening and hair-flicking. Dance music blared from a massive speaker next to our table and, of course, Paul was next to me, his puppy eyes slaveringly following my every move. I drank quickly and determinedly. I drank to get drunk. Champagne bottles appeared like magic and I didn't question where they came from. Sitting opposite Enrique, I didn't dare to look at his face too often, but I stared at his hands. His long lean fingers were graceful like those of a dancer and I noticed that he wore an obscenely expensive watch. Emma draped herself over him constantly and giggled into his ear.

 Paul and Zoe sat either side of me like bookends. Paul constantly leaning in and trying to engage me with some inane remark. Zoe stared fixedly at the dance floor, her expression stony, the make-up mask growing harsher with the passing of time and inebriation. Drunk disco hours. Eventually it all became a flashing blur. Periodically, we went off to dance. Zoe and Paul seemed to be my designated partners. Zoe would jog unhappily from side to side. I was pretty drunk and lurching about. People were staring at me and men leaned in and said things. I didn't understand them. Back at the table, Paul started retching. His eyes wide and horrified, his face translucent and blotchy. Zoe grabbed his skinny wrist and dragged him clumsily to the back, where the toilets were. I stared at the dance floor. The lights were swimming about. Opposite me, Emma and Enrique were snogging, his arm draped languidly around her shoulders, his fingers still holding a lit cigarette. It was a sex tableau but I was careful not to stare.

Sometime later, tequila came.

Later still, I felt sick too, suddenly. Bile rose violently in my throat. I staggered towards the toilets, everything spinning. The cubicles were occupied and I vomited into a sink. I heard outraged Spanish expressions of disgust all around me but I didn't care because I felt instantly better.

Exiting the ladies, I literally bumped into Enrique who must have been coming out of the men's. I couldn't really control my body at that point. I felt fluid, like an octopus. He put his arms around me, both arms, to steady me. He smelt so good, so expensive. I leant my head against his shoulder for just one second before he let go, gently pushing me away without comment, moving on. Directly behind him was Zoe looming with her ghoulish made-up face flickering in the strobe lights.

"I came to see if you were alright?"

Her eyebrows were raised and her tone had something unpleasant in it.

"I guess that you can handle yourself," she snorted, "Of course, I knew that already!"

The night wound down, messily. Paul was legless and had to be carried. I don't remember if anyone spoke. The music obliterated everything. In the car, Paul, surprisingly weighty, lay across us in the back seat. He stank of sweat and vomit and cheap aftershave. I felt crushed by his weight and a little desperate to get out of there. Exhaustion and nausea suffocated me.

Fortunately, they dropped me home first.

I stayed in bed the whole of the following day feeling sick and sorry for myself. I dreamt of Enrique in a disjointed way. Partially lust but mainly a longing to be held. I felt as if there was something about the previous night that I should remember but whatever it was flickered at my subconscious and then evaporated.

Chapter 7

Emma took the following week off work too. I didn't see Zoe and Paul before they flew back home. I was quite relieved in all honesty. I didn't find anything ominous about it. Of course, I should have done. It was obviously weird that Paul, having made a fuss about seeing me once, would not try and engineer another outing.

Work carried on as before. I hung out with Penny, ignored the other gringos, chatted to my students. Every so often, the dark one, Ed, would acknowledge me in a grudging way as if annoyed that I was still there but proud of himself for his magnanimity. He probably thought of himself as a good bloke.

Penny told me that the Americans that came to DF, to Mexico in general, were often escaping something back home. Either something that had been done to them, or in the case of the blokes, more often, something which they had done.

"Even something illegal?" I asked, horrified

"Sure!" she laughed drily. We were drinking beer again. It was mid-afternoon on a Friday.

"Why not? All they have to do is get across the border and not go back! Unless they are some real hotshot criminals, no one is going to come looking for them. Mainly, they're just common and garden thugs."

I ordered a couple more beers and thought about the reedy pathetic specimens in the staff room.

"I don't reckon any of the blokes we work with are master criminals."

"They're shits though," she took a great swig, "I bet they're escaping from something."

"I'd love to know what!" I mused.

"Well…" she grinned in a sly way.

"Well, what? You know something don't you? What? Go on, you've got to tell me!"

"I don't know…" she feigned reluctance, pretending to fiddle with the label on her beer.

"Come on! Don't pretend you have any loyalty towards those arseholes!"

She laughed loudly then, "Of course not! I'm just winding you up!"

"Well, what then…which one, is it that Ed? he's the biggest tosser in my opinion!"

"OK," she leaned forward towards me with and carried on in a loud dramatic whisper, "I may have overheard Stefan talking to Ed in his office… there was some discrepancy with his visa, some issue. I honestly couldn't really hear everything, but the issue seemed to be that Ed has a criminal record in the States!"

"Ohhh, what for?" I sensed, behind my curiosity, the purest of happiness, just for one instant.

"I don't know, I was listening through the door, I couldn't go up and put my ear against it!"

"I bet it was something to do with women, he strikes me as a real misogynist arsehole."

She lit a cigarette and inhaled deeply, pretending to contemplate the steady stream of traffic.

"Well…I did hear Stefan say that he would give him a chance, but any reports of inappropriate behaviour and he would be out."

"See! Knew it! It's something to do with women! Stefan wouldn't take that risk if it was kids!"

"Ed never does the kid classes though…"

"Oh, yes, that is true." It was a sobering thought and we stopped laughing abruptly. Twice a week there was an afternoon kids' class and me, Penny and Emma took turns to teach it. The kids were spoilt and annoying. I had presumed that Stefan chose the women to teach it as we were supposed to be more nurturing. Now, I suspected that there may be a more sinister reason.

One night, my dad phoned. He had been calling about once a month and we would have quite a superficial chat about food, usually, and sometimes I would tell him some anecdotes about my students. This conversation felt very different though.

He started by asking me when I was coming home. As soon as he asked, I realised that deep down I wanted to return home straight away. I wanted to put an end to this loneliness. Because in spite of my blossoming friendship with Penny, I realised that I was still lonely. At least I knew that my family loved me, even though they weren't particularly demonstrative. On the other hand, I didn't want to look like a failure. I felt like I should at least stick it out for twelve months, maybe travel around too. In general, I thought that I should make an effort to behave like a normal gap year kid. I told my dad, that I was thinking I would return around June. There was silence on the line. I could hear him breathing. I lit a cigarette and worry crawled into my brain.

"Your mother has left." he said then in a strangled voice. He spoke so quietly that I could barely hear him. "This morning, she left."

"What?" I barked, incredulous.

He repeated himself, but even then, I understood that he meant that she had gone out somewhere, like she often did. She was a real social butterfly. She hadn't ever liked to stay in, not for as long as I could remember.

"She's gone off with that bloke from her office." He sounded as if he was choking.

With encroaching horror, I realised that he was crying.

"What bloke?" I asked stupidly.

"Apparently, it's been going on for years. I had no bloody idea, did you?"

There was silence. I couldn't think fast enough.

"Did you? Did you know about it?" He sounded louder, desperate.

"Dad calm down! I had no idea, of course not! I don't believe it!"

"Of course not, love, I'm sorry. I just don't know. I don't know what to do."

"What bloke from the office?"

I couldn't picture anyone from my mum's office apart from a chubby friend of my hers called Mandy who had a loud annoying laugh. I wasn't even totally sure what my mum did, some kind of secretarial, administrative thing. I knew that it was an insurance office. Very boring and unsexy. I couldn't imagine anything nefarious going on there.

"Some bloke, Jack, Jake, something like that. He started years ago, fuck! Years! It's been going on for years!"

"You don't know that dad…" I lit another cigarette, nervously, from the dregs of the last one.

"She had to mentor him. Mentor him! The bastard!"

I didn't know what else to say, I felt all my words leave me, like the smoke seeping out of my mouth. I needed to talk to my brother but I was aware that he was painfully immature and also that neither of us were equipped for either this situation or for any conversation that we should have about it.

As if reading my mind then my dad sighed deeply and said;

"I have to tell your brother. How do I tell your brother?"

"Where is he?"

"He's in his room. He's got his music playing, he can't hear anything."

"Get him, I'll talk to him!"

"No, love, it's alright, I'll do it."

"No, seriously, let me dad."

"It shouldn't be down to you."

I suddenly couldn't bear it any longer, any of it.

"Just get him, dad, please."

"OK love." he sounded defeated.

I heard muffled footsteps and then the tigerish leaps of my hyperactive brother.

"Alright, Abs?"

"Hi Si, are you OK?"

"What's up? Dad said you wanted to talk to me?"

He sounded so bouncy; I didn't know how to tell him. I lit a third cigarette. My throat felt dry and raspy. I shifted uncomfortably on the hard tiles.

"Hello?" he trilled in an irritating sing-song voice which would normally have driven me mad.

"Mum's left." I stated abruptly.

"What?"

"She's left with some bloke from work."

"Don't be fucking ridiculous, you're in Mexico, how could you possibly know that?"

"Dad just told me, you idiot."
"Well he would have told me if it was true."

"He wanted me to tell you. It is true, I'm sorry."

He became shouty and angry. I could picture him leaping off the walls, his limbs wiry and lethal.

"He asked me to tell you." I tried to sound as patient as possible, to remember that he was young, mentally young. "I don't know why."

I felt my nose drip. Tears ran down my cheeks. Silence on the line.

Then dad's voice, subdued.

"Thanks, love."

"What's he doing?"

"He's gone back into his room."
I could hear, even long distant, the loud dull thud of his music.

"I'll come home dad." I said, truthfully relieved to have an excuse.

"No love!" he sounded panicked, then.

"I don't want you to cut short your year abroad for me!"

"Ok, don't worry, we'll talk about it another time."

I realised that he wanted to believe in the cheerful gap year narrative for me, but also for himself, even though he must have known, deep down, that it was fiction.

We planned to talk more often. He was going to find out where my mum was and try to talk to her calmly. I didn't hold out much hope.

In my head I started counting down until June. I wish that I had left then. If I had gone back home then, everything would have been different.

Chapter 8

At work the next day, I told Penny all about it. We were sitting in the staffroom speaking in low voices but she put a finger to her lips and I realised that Ed was right behind me, pretending to read a grammar book, obviously eavesdropping. We stopped talking then and resumed after work, in our now habitual spot in the outdoor food market. Quesadillas sat steaming before me but I had no appetite. I had struggled to eat anything since the conversation with my dad.

"You poor love," said Penny, "I wonder why she left."

"What?"

"Why your mum left."
I realised then that Penny was observing this saga from the perspective of the abused wife. I almost laughed, half-snorted instead. I couldn't imagine anything more unlikely and ludicrous than my dad abusing my mum.

"She had an affair!" I raised my voice abruptly and people looked at us.

"She's the villain here! It happens you know!"
Penny chewed her lunch slowly, looking sceptical. Suddenly and for the first time, she annoyed me, got on my nerves. I couldn't stand to watch her eat any longer. I jumped up; quesadillas untouched.

"See you tomorrow!" I shouted over my shoulders and jogged off.

"Abby! Abby! Wait!"

But, in that instant, I couldn't face her or anyone else.

I started walking, just putting one foot in front of the other. I passed the metro stop into which I usually descended, like a rat into its hole. I kept going, smoking one cigarette after another, lungs burning and sour. Acid churning in my empty stomach. I had become used to monitoring who was around me but I was so enraged and miserable that I let my guard down. I noticed men staring, of course, out of the corner of my eye. They were always staring. It was so commonplace that it had become unremarkable. Ditto the whistling and hissing and low creepy calling; "Mamacita! Mamacita!" I didn't notice this particular man following me though, and as soon as I did, I was furious with myself. I had learnt, through bitter experience, that you had to disappear from the stalkers straightaway. My strategy was either to go into a shop and engage some old man or lady in a trumped-up conversation, usually to do with being a lost gringo, or, if there were no suitable shops, to outrun them. But this guy was right behind me. He was squat and burly and he was wearing a baseball cap pulled down over his face. He had obviously been inching closer and closer whilst I was engrossed in my unhappy thoughts. A mere second after I had finally noticed him, and also registered that there were no shops on the residential street which we were on, he grabbed my arm. I tried to shake him off, but I couldn't. His grip was very strong. My stomach dipped, I felt icy sweat drench me. I shook and struggled but he started dragging me down the street. People stared but then quickly lowered their heads, obviously not wanting to get involved. They even got out of his way! His hand was like a vice on my arm. Everything I knew about self-defence was useless in this instance. I couldn't get my nails into his eyeballs. I couldn't knee him in the balls. I couldn't bite him or bend his finger back. I was in the wrong position for all of it. He stank of something rancid. I shouted, my voice reedy and thin. Like a nightmare when no one can hear you. "Help! Help!" It didn't seem to help at all.

People just looked away.

I was crying and sobbing, I was losing hope. I was cursing my decision to ever come to this stupid city. Suddenly, his grip loosened. I whipped my head round and saw that a man had grabbed my assailant. A much larger, also sinister looking man, solid as a body builder. He was holding him in a headlock and a crowd gathered then. My arm slumped and then throbbed in pain. Through blurry tears, I saw the grubby crowd with their alien faces and their hooded, unknowable expressions, devoid of empathy, that's what I thought. Maybe paranoid, maybe not. I ran and ran and ran. I ran so hard that I felt daggers pierce my lungs. Amazingly, I was much closer to home than I had thought. I had run through an area which was completely unfamiliar to me, not even a terrible area, just non-descript.

At home, I lay on the tiled floor panting. My clothes were drenched with cooling sweat. I decided to return to the UK immediately, as soon as I could. Once I had made that decision, I felt calm and composed. It seemed like the most logical decision in the world, I lit a cigarette still lying on the floor and watched the smoke drift through sunbeams. My heartbeat slowed and, weirdly, I felt myself drifting into a pre-sleep haze, right there with my head resting on the stone tiles.

The calm radiated through me like a drug, it infused my body.

The next day at school, I told Penny that I was leaving. She seemed anxious to forget our minor disagreement and was effusively friendly and warm.

"Oh no, that's so sad!" she cried, "You haven't seen any of the great parts of Mexico, just worked here in this shithole!"

"That's OK." I mumbled placidly. I felt massively relieved now that the decision had been made. I was really looking forward to going home and to trying to sort out the mess with my mum.

"It's not really OK, is it! It's supposed to be your 'gap year', isn't that what you Brits call it? Seriously, working here? That's it?!You won't have much of a story to tell when you're older, will you?"

Emma walked in then. I hadn't seen her since the night at the club. Even at work, she seemed to be avoiding me. I had the slight suspicion that me falling on Enrique, (which was how I remembered it, as a 'falling') would have been twisted by Zoe into a conscious seduction on my part with malevolent intent.

Apparently not though. Emma gave me a huge friendly grin as she joined the conversation.

"Oh totally, we can't have you leaving Mexico without at least trying out Acapulco, the gringo paradise!"

Even more weirdly, then, Ed joined in.

"My favourite place! If you're going to Acapulco, count me in!"

The other two girls were just as shocked as me. We all stared at him. There was a bewildered silence. Penny and I exchanged glances as we both remembered, uncomfortably, everything that she had told me about him.

"We'll get Enrique to drive us!" Emma concluded.

So that seemed to be a plan. Even then I didn't really want to go. No, I didn't want to go at all, but I did feel that they were right. My gap year had been pretty uninspiring so far, I should at least do something supposedly fun. I reluctantly agreed.

A long weekend in Acapulco and then I'd fly home. Little did I know.

Chapter 9

I called my dad to find out how he was and to give him an update. He sounded resigned and old and sad. He said that he was so terrified of bumping into my mum in town or at the supermarket that he never left the house except to go to work at the bank. He had been a bank clerk his whole life. He sent my brother to the shops which I imagine was a world of pain for both of them.

I told him that I was returning home really soon. He tried to talk me out of it again but I could tell that he was really happy. His complaints were half-hearted and he was excited about me visiting Acapulco.

"I've always wanted to go there you know?" he enthused, "That used to be where all the rich gangsters ended up."

As he said that I was reminded once again of my narrow escape on the grubby streets just around the corner, but there was no reason to burden him with that. He was suffering enough.

I told him I'd call again to tell him my flight details.

Before I left for Acapulco, the day before, when I was packing my small backpack, Elena came into my room, uncharacteristically, and sat on my bed. She still looked business-like in her work suit and heels. To me, that outfit spoke of great discomfort.

"OK." she said when I told her my plans. She looked worried. "Be careful, you know, roads are bad."

I thought she meant that people drove like nutters. That isn't what she meant, but it would be too late before I worked that out. At the time, I just nodded and grinned like a fool and thanked her for hosting me. She made me write out my home number in the UK and stuck it with a magnet onto the fridge. I found this oddly touching.

They picked me up in Enrique's car late afternoon on Friday. The plan had been to escape the rush hour traffic but what with one delay and another, it didn't work out like that. By the time they collected me, everyone was already sitting in the car, still shiny, sleek and dark as a predator. I jostled into the back seat. Penny and Ed were also there, Penny in the seat nearest to me and it was odd seeing them outside of work and out of context. They never dressed up to teach, nobody did, but now they were wearing clothes that I had never seen before. Penny was wearing a yellow sundress. The straps dug into her flesh and her flaxen hair was loose and puffy over her shoulders. The back seat was wide but she was a hefty girl and must have been uncomfortable sitting in the middle. Nevertheless, she turned to give me a wide smile and bizarrely, so did Ed. I didn't trust it though. He had never smiled at me before and it looked like a grimace, his pink gums were clearly visible. Enrique and Emma largely ignored me. There was a dismissive, muted 'Hi' and a superficial hand wave, but I saw Enrique's eyes in the mirror watch me. There was scrutiny in them. They were cold and for some reason worry came and hovered over me.

It took us an age to get out of Mexico City. Our senses were drugged and toxic with all the traffic fumes as we crawled along, bumper to bumper. By the time we hit the Autopista del Sol, it was a massive relief. The space and speed of the open road was exhilarating. The sun was setting across open swathes of desert. It felt dramatic and peaceful. Enrique played ambient music and the sun washed over me, lulling me into a false sense of security. I didn't realise that it was a misguided sense at the time. The car glided smoothly down the highway. I felt a glimmer of happiness or if not exactly happiness, I felt that at last I was doing the right thing, the expected thing. This kind of thing was exactly what gap year kids were expected to do. They went on adventures with friends. Penny was certainly my friend, although I had grave doubts, even misgivings, about the others. Enrique was something. Not necessarily anything good and certainly not a friend, but something.

Penny and I chatted in low voices beneath the rhythm of the music. Our disagreement over my mum leaving had been forgotten and our conversation was amiable. Ed stared out of the window, his head nodding gormlessly to the beat. He looked weedy and defenceless, incapable of violence. His thin white arms were folded into his lap. He no longer looked like the sarcastic, malevolent ogre from the staffroom. The sunset reflected in our faces and we were all pink and glowing. We had some bottles of beer with us and the mood in the back seat grew gregarious and pleasant. Even Ed chatted, albeit in a stilted way. Emma and Enrique rarely turned towards the back however. They spoke in very low voices to each other, practically whispers. He drove with his slim hand laid on her lap, his other hand splayed across the steering wheel, elongated fingers, they looked oddly powerful. At some point, we needed to pee after all that beer and we pulled off the side of the highway into a modern service station. It looked shiny and newly built. We had to pay for the facilities but they were spotless and modern. We bought more beers and by the time we arrived at the congested suburbs around Acapulco, stuck in traffic again, we were all happily drunk in the back seat. The night was humid and lit with interesting visual displays. Run down slums with ramshackle lighting gave way to beaming modern hotel complexes. There were people everywhere, perched outside the rundown shacks or buying street food. A loud cacophony of music blared from all angles.

We had rented a basic bungalow-type shack next to the beach. It was not on the main strip, obviously, but at right angles to the bay in a poorer suburb. I was feeling a bit sick by the time that we finally arrived. I hadn't eaten in ages and more than anything I craved some food and a sleep. Fortunately, the others were hungry as well. Enrique and Emma who seemed a unit apart from us, always, went to buy some food. They returned with a stack of tortas, more beers and a bottle of tequila. We sat on some plastic chairs on a makeshift concrete patio in front of our bungalow. The air smelled of the sea. The ocean smashed against the sand before us and muted sounds of traffic and distant music come from behind, from the town. It was very dark and Emma lit huge candles in jars which were supposed to ward off mosquitoes. I guessed that she had brought them with her and lulled by exhaustion and beer, I marvelled at her foresight and efficiency. I shared a tiny, smelly room with Penny. We had a mattress each, a sheet and a thin cover. It felt quite intimate.

Someone, not me, had a polaroid camera and I recall seeing a few snaps of me from that time.

There I was chatting with Penny, the candle like an exploding flame illuminating my face, I had a beer in one hand and a cigarette in another. My face looked blank and guileless. I looked really young. Another photo was of us all leaning against Enrique's car. We weren't slumped, we were posing. We held the ubiquitous beers and cigarettes, our hips jutted out, our sunburnt limbs looked smooth and youthful. We looked drunk and happy. Only Enrique had turned away. Perhaps he was annoyed that we were leaning on his car.

But that happened on the next day.

That first night and on the subsequent nights there I slept so deeply. I slept as if I was drugged and, in the mornings, I would struggle to open my eyes.

I remember that it was fun. We ran into the ocean and we drank beer. We constructed a makeshift fire on the beach and made plans to grill meat but no one knew what they were doing so instead we bought big puffy American marshmallows and roasted them on sticks until they were burnt and dripping. Someone hung a lopsided hammock between two palm trees and we took turns pretending that it was comfortable.

On the last evening, Sunday, we drove to the main strip in Acapulco and in one tacky, crowded bar watched beautiful, intoxicated American girls parade in wet t-shirts on a stage, in front of jeering groups of men, boys, they all looked predatory. All three of us girls were offended and walked out, but the boys stayed for longer, their eyes wide and greedy. We waited for them outside. Penny and I were a bit drunk and chatting normally, but Emma was even more monosyllabic than usual.

We went to a club then and bought one cocktail each. Only one because they were so expensive but they must have been very strong because that night was a blur of dancing. I seem to recall being on a podium with Penny at some point! Men kept grabbing me and Penny would try to intervene and then they were grabbing her too. In the end, we had had enough and we huddled in a dark corner waiting for the others to wind down and to want to leave.

On Monday, there was a massive grey rain cloud like an ominous blot on the sun.

Chapter 10

All day we felt ill. We were hungover and nauseous. We lay in the hammock or on the sand. It was really humid and the sky was heavy with rain. It felt like the heavens were waiting for a signal to unleash the full force of their rage.

I had thought that Ed was friendlier on that trip. He had hung out more with me and Penny. I was beginning to think that Penny must have been mistaken about what she had overheard. He seemed too reedy to be capable of anything criminal. However, on that last day he distanced himself. He sat right by the water's edge with his feet in the sea, staring at it. His back was sunburnt. He looked kind of mournful and I felt pity for him, I remember that.

At around 6pm we packed up. Emma insisted that we all had one last drink, 'a goodbye Acapulco cocktail' she called it and spent some time in the tiny kitchen mixing it together. It had vodka and peach juice in it and was thick and sweet. We all smiled goofily and toasted each other and a bit self-consciously said 'Goodbye Acapulco'. I started looking forward properly to going home. There was nothing else standing in my way and I couldn't wait to get on the plane.

I worried a bit about Enrique driving, he had drunk very little of the cocktail but he seemed exhausted and out of sorts. Neither him nor Emma had spoken much to me or Penny the entire weekend. A few times, I thought he was watching me though from behind his sunglasses and I would get goosebumps.

It started to rain almost as soon as we set off and the traffic was slow going exiting Acapulco. Some of the roads in the suburbs were little more than dirt tracks, and in the rain, they became slick and slippery with muddy puddles. Cars inched through them, bumper to bumper, painfully slowly. The torrential rain didn't hit us until we were on the highway and I felt worried by the lack of visibility and by the speed of the cars. I felt really sleepy suddenly and then I must have drifted off. When I opened my eyes again, it had completely stopped raining. We were on a mud road parked outside, what looked like, a rudimentary petrol station with one rusty pump and a tiny shack behind it. Penny, next to me, must have slept too and was rubbing her eyes. I felt suddenly violently sick and dizzy. I struggled to speak.

"Why did we leave the highway?" I asked

Nobody looked at me, but I heard Emma's voice, it seemed fuzzy, wobbly.

"Oh, we needed petrol."

Puzzled, I recalled the slick, modern petrol station from before and then felt an overwhelming urge to vomit. It felt like the food poisoning all over again.

"I'm going to be sick." I groaned.

"Me too." moaned Penny who was crumpled next to me.

Emma turned to us then. I remember that. It was the first time that she had looked me in the face all weekend and her eyes were bright and excited. She looked radiant, pretty. I remember thinking, we all ate the same food, why didn't she feel sick?

"There's a toilet just behind that building." she said smoothly.

We must have looked sceptical because she added quickly;

"It's Ok actually. I've just been."
There was no choice. Of course, later I realised that they had removed that choice. Vomit was rising up in me like a flood and apparently Penny felt the same way. We stumbled out of the car disorientated and dizzy. There was a roar in my ears, a

malfunction. We staggered to the building, which looked like a ramshackle shack, its windows were murky. We leaned against the walls and inched our way around to look for the toilet. I felt so dizzy, I thought that I may faint at any moment.

When we arrived behind the hut, we just stared in total dismay.

There was nothing there at all, just desert and rocks. The ground was still damp from the rain. Realisation started to trickle through our brains then like venom, but before we could think vomit took over. Back- to- back, we leant forward, vomiting copiously. Our hands on our knees, bent forward, shaking and ill and weak. Finally spent, I lay on the ground, close to unconsciousness and clearly, the thought came: We had been poisoned. Whatever they had given us must have been slightly hallucinogenic because we seemed to have lost all concept of time. Noone came for us, as I knew by then that they wouldn't, and it was Penny, who finally managed to gather her strength, such as it was, and inch her way back around the building to be confronted by nothing. Just an empty space. Of course, they had driven away and left us there.

It was unbearable, like a sudden punch in the gut but also completely logical, almost inevitable. Emma hated me and this was her revenge. Like a joke but crucially, not a joke.

I opened my eyes and saw Penny's desperate, frantic face.

"They've gone, GONE!" she wailed.

I grabbed her sweaty hand to acknowledge to her that I was there, but I was drifting out of consciousness again. Whatever they had slipped into our drinks was stronger than me.

"Why would they do that?" I heard her incredulity and despair and then I faded out again.

I came to behind a spindly tree, still behind the building. I felt clearer albeit still shaky and Penny offered me a sip of water.

"Just a sip, this is all we have." It was one of those mid-sized bottles of water. She must have managed to grab it as she scrambled out of the car. It was literally the only thing we had. We were in just our clothes. I had a sweatshirt tied round my shoulders. We were both wearing shorts and t-shirts. The rain had completely cleared and a beautiful clear sky was hung with stars. There was no sound but the discordant chirping of a million insects. Our clothes against our clammy bodies felt chilly. We got up carefully, still very shaky and walked tentatively and silently around the front of the building and confirmed what, really, we already knew. The building was deserted and derelict and the road in front of it was not a road but a dirt track. They had deviated deliberately. Our blurry drugged eyes traced the rough winding snake of the track through the lifeless swathe of land. Desert. Cactus. Rock.

I turned to Penny. We were sitting then, leaning against the building. The roar of a desert silence hung heavy in the air.

"We have to conserve our energy, that's the only way that we'll survive this!" She had been crying continuously for hours at that point, I could see it in her swollen red eyes. A thought came; we have to stay hydrated; we could die here.

"We don't know how long we will be here," I added, "Before they turn back to get us…"

"Turn back!" she spat at me, almost with venom.

"They're not turning back! Are you mad? This was it, deliberate, they had planned to do this all along. To you! They wanted to get to you! I was just, was just collateral…" she gasped, heaving with sobs.

"I was just collateral damage." she ran out of steam and sat breathing heavily, her head down.

"Your so-called 'friend'!" she added bitterly, as an afterthought, and then was silent.

At that time, she was still ahead of me. I was still too weak, too unwell, to think it through. Too confused to work out the whys and wherefores.

"That's what Ed was for!" she shouted, suddenly.

My mind whirling, I gazed at the horror in her face.

"What?"

Behind her the sky blinked with the unappreciated beauty of a thousand stars.

"They must have paid him to help them!"

"What?"

"That little shit will do anything for money, they roped him in, easy!"

I wanted to tell her to calm down, to conserve her strength. I couldn't cope with all the dreadful information at that moment, I felt myself drifting off again.

"Don't cry!" I mumbled and I put my head on her shoulder and fell asleep to the sound of her outraged sobs. The ground was hard and unyielding beneath us.

I awoke to the sunrise blazing pink over the desert. It was beautiful. My throat felt so dry and scratchy. Penny was awake already and told me;

"I stayed awake all night. I kept watch."

Her tone was accusing so I thanked her. I didn't dare ask for more water, although the dryness in my throat was now pain. She told me that she hadn't seen anything but she had heard the distant cries of something wild, maybe coyotes? We couldn't remember which animals resided in this desert. Anyway, I still didn't have the energy to think.

"Someone is bound to come…" I whispered and urged her to go to sleep, she looked dreadful.

"I will keep guard." I promised, my voice a low croak.

Through that interminable morning, I forced myself to stay awake whilst Penny slept on the ground, her head on my sweatshirt, now stained and grimy. I leant against the wall. There was nothing to focus on except desert and sky, the glaring sun, the buzz of insects. We were in the partial shade of the building, of our one spindly tree.

She woke when the sun was directly overhead and immediately stared accusingly at the water bottle;

"Did you drink this?"

I had had the teeniest sip. My throat was so dry. It was half-full.

"No!" I insisted but I could tell that she didn't believe me.

Another twenty-four hours passed in a similar fashion, in pain, half-dreaming. By then we were

so depleted that we slept together on the ground, unable to keep our eyes open. I dreamt of my mum. In my feverish dreams she was roaming the desert with Enrique, hand in hand. Sometimes out of the corner of my eye, I thought that I could see the sleek predatory silhouette of Enrique's car but it was just a mirage.

"We're going to die here." mumbled Penny and her voice could barely be heard, her lips were so cracked, they looked like pain. I wanted it to be over at that point. My throat burned. The water was gone.

Then the men came. It was an interminable amount of time later and we could no longer move. The men stood over us and blotted out the sun. I could barely see, there were shapes everywhere, floaters. I thought it was Enrique and Ed and the other gringo from Elite, repentant and come to rescue us. Then I heard Penny near me, whimper in fear and I knew that my supposition had been wrong and that it was worse than that, much worse. It didn't even matter, not then. For me, anyway, things had stopped mattering. They hoisted us up like sacks of flour, like Christmas presents, I was hallucinating. One grabbed me. Two took Penny, heftier, between them. My eyes were sealed shut but the one who was carrying me stank. He stank to high heaven, of ingrained sweat and filth.

We were deposited on the back of a pick- up truck and covered with a blanket, blissfully dark and musty and then there was the sound of Mexican dialect, guttural and rough. However, I also realised that their voices were young, that they were younger than I had presumed. The engine started. They set off down the rocky dirt track and instinctively, we put our hands under our heads to stop them banging against the metal floor. Much time passed. My sunburnt skin was battered repeatedly by bouncing around the base of the truck, my throat was swollen and painful. Through interminable hours, they drove us. I struggled to hear other cars, other evidence of civilisation but I just heard them, only them, their excitable voices and the tinny sound of a cheap radio. Every so often my body would jolt and collide with Penny's soft flesh and we would both whimper. We were like trussed sheep being taken to market.

I must have passed out again, When I came too, I could hear Penny whimpering and crying and I was being dragged out of the truck, feet first, the skin of my whole body scratched and dry and aching. I realised that we were under the canopy of the night. There were sounds in the near vicinity, a cacophony of chirping crickets, and behind them the roar of traffic and also distant voices. Our captors were whispering so must have been worried about being overheard. We were in the outskirts of a town or a village, that was my guess. Illogically, I felt optimistic. In my confused state, I reasoned that it was better than before, alone in the desert because there were people here and people wouldn't let us die. That was when I heard Penny shout and then the harsh crack of a slap on skin, a muffled choking. Something foul and soft was shoved into my mouth. I gagged, kept gagging, couldn't spit it out, my hands were tied. Hoisted over a shoulder again, I saw the back of my captor's dirty jeans. He was so thin, I wondered how he could lift me, diminished though I was. We were dragged down a concrete passage and taken to a room like a cell. It was a cell. It had one squalid double mattress and a naked bulb. There were no windows. We were deposited unceremoniously on the mattress, first me and then I felt it give and saw Penny there. Her face was streaked red in the light of the bulb and her mouth was stuffed with what looked like a sock. Her eyes were wild, like those of a deranged person. A key turned in the heavy door, there was the sound of a bolt being dragged across. Their footsteps receded. They had untied us, we took the filthy socks out of our mouths and held each other. Initially, our hearts banging in our chests, that was all that we could think to do.

"They haven't killed us yet, at least," sobbed Penny into my neck, "but they will."

Her tears were drenching me. I wanted to say "conserve your energy" but the words would not come.

Footsteps. The door unlocked with a scrape and two big bottles of water were thrown in by a disembodied arm. The door relocked. I have never before, nor since, known such relief, such pure animal joy as when I gulped down that water. I drank a quarter then stopped and grabbed Penny's shoulder. It was lukewarm, stale, but tasted of heaven.

"Ration it!" I gasped at her; my face drenched. The disgusting mattress was soggy around me where the water had splashed.

Reluctantly, she put her bottle down.

We felt better, calmer, more alert.

"What do they want?"

"Money, of course!"

"How? We don't have any?"

"A ransom probably, via the government. They'll try to get to our families."

"My family doesn't have any money."

"Mine neither. They don't care. They think that all gringos have money."

I knew better than to point out that I was not a gringo.

Chapter 11

Some time passed and the door flung open. We started, grabbed each other, sweat and panic. One of them was standing there, lanky, filthy blue jeans falling off his hips, wearing a black rudimentary mask; a stocking with the eyes cut out. Almost lazily, in one skinny hand, he dangled a gun. In the other hand was a paper bag which he threw at us. It landed on the mattress and we stared at it suspiciously, we didn't approach it.

"Is food!" he shouted at us, in English and left, slamming the door. We grabbed at the bag, both together. It was a loaf of bread, still quite soft. We attacked it like animals, like the coyotes in the desert. Then, stuffed and bloated with bread we slept, the single light bulb still glaring above us. We had no way of knowing, as the hours passed and we existed in a sickly, almost surreal dream state, if it was day or night.

Time kept moving on, perhaps days, we did not know. They did not tell us, initially, what they wanted from us. The same guy, with the mask and the gun, would throw food and water at us periodically. Mostly it was bread, sometimes a rock-hard cake, occasionally, a slab of cheese. We demolished it all. We started to feel better, not normal obviously, but much better than we had in the desert, strength shakily returning to our limbs.

After too long, the same boy/man would come in to empty the disgusting bucket in the corner, our rudimentary toilet.

Mainly, we were too exhausted and terrified to talk but occasionally, in furious whispers, we would wonder aloud about who would miss us. "My dad" I'd say, or sometimes "my brother". That's it. That's all I had. I didn't feel as if I could rely on my mum any longer. She was loping off somewhere, with unknown men, flinging careless goodbyes over her shoulder like petals into the wind.

Penny would say her parents, maybe, but she hadn't spoken to them in years. They'd been furious when she'd left Jesse. In their small town, in their tight-knit community, that just wasn't done. It was not the done thing, you put up and shut up.

"I wonder what they would think of me if they saw me now…" she mused bitterly

Our lips were less cracked, our throats were less dry but in the harsh artificial light we faced each other like ghouls.

Days passed, probably, and then three of them came at once. All of them with the ridiculous masks, two of them dangling small revolvers from their skinny fingers. They looked like children playing, not fully grown. We weren't as afraid of them as we should have been. The one without the gun had a notepad and a biro. He was taller, leaner and looked the most agitated. Also, and this struck me as a surprising detail: he was barefoot and his toenails were filthy.

"Address!" he shouted at us and we jumped, jerked from sitting to standing, our arms entwined, holding each other up.

"Name! Address!"

Penny took a deep breath and said something soothing in Spanish. He shouted back at us.

"He wants the contact details for our families."

She turned to me with the same soothing voice.

"What do we do?" I was panicking and shaking.

I kept picturing my dad's face, how stricken he would be.

"We just do it. We give them what they want. There's nothing else that we can do, what choice do we have!"

I looked at the man with the notebook and he shouted at me.

"Don't look at him or he'll have to shoot you." said Penny in the same smooth, hypnotic tone of voice. "That's what he is saying. That's good by the way." she muttered as we wrote out our addresses in the notebook, our handwriting shaky and uneven.

"Good!?" I spluttered, too loudly

"Shhh. Yes, good. If they were planning on killing us, they wouldn't mind if we saw their faces, it wouldn't make a difference."

"Oh." I felt a sinking sensation as the logic of what she was saying hit me. My legs gave way and I sank on to the mattress. I stayed there, dizzy and weak.

They left and Penny joined me on the mattress. We had run out of things to say a while ago. Mainly we just lay there. Sometimes we fantasized about food. This time she stroked my hair in a maternal way.

"It's going to be alright you know." She stated. As if to prove her point one of our captors returned a few hours later struggling under the bulk of an old TV set. The kind that you would see in charity shops in the UK. He put it down and then went out again and returned with a crate, onto which he put the TV. He fiddled with it, his gun in his back pocket. It wasn't the barefoot one. This one looked so lean, so adolescent, the gun resembled a toy. At one point he brushed past me and I could have grabbed it.

There was static and then suddenly, loudly, the TV spluttered into life. It was showing, what looked like, a Mexican drama of some kind, a soap opera. Our hearts still racing, we sat on our mattress and watched. Eventually, as one soap opera blended into another, they created a soporific effect. I didn't understand the dialogue, obviously, but I became transfixed by the flamboyant sets and costumes, even the obviously terrible acting.

"Why the TV do you think?" I asked Penny.

"To calm us down? I don't know, it's working, isn't it?"

"Huh, clever!" I snorted

"They're not evil, you know," she mused, "just poor."

I looked at her.

"This is commonplace here. It is almost all they know."

"If they were evil, they wouldn't have left us the TV."

We looked at each other and grinned suddenly, stupidly. Her teeth were very grey.

I thought about it then. They were clearly impoverished, Penny was right. This was not evil, from their perspective. Evil had come before when Emma and Enrique had deliberately left us to be picked off the street like road kill.

More days went past. We could trace them now because of the scheduling of the TV programmes. At midnight, broadcasting stopped and resumed at 6am. The TV became as a friend, a gregarious, chatty companion. I started picking up whole sentences of Spanish. We bickered about the characters in the soap operas. It is true that everyone can eventually adapt to anything. We were beyond filthy and our new home was a stinking pit but we were distracted.

Plus, they fed us more. Sometimes whole meals arrived in takeout containers with hot chilli on the side. Sometimes we even forgot to fear our child captors. I don't know if we were drugged. If the unbranded cola drink was spiked. Certainly, we were sleepy, low-level fatigued the entire time. Our teeth, of course, felt revolting. I could practically feel them rotting in my head. We never completely got used to the stench, either: the toilet bucket, our unwashed bodies, the rancid clothes. We largely became immune to it but it sat there engulfing us like a mushroom cloud. Our filthy faces swamped by the lurid colours on the screen, waiting through the hours for our young captors to throw food at us. We were just like animals, inured to captivity.

Chapter 12

Then, there was the day of the shouting. Usually, our lives there were quiet, punctuated by the static and the voices on the TV, turned low. The shouting was loud and just outside the walls. First there was just yelling, colourful Mexican curses. Followed by the sound of rapidly running footsteps and then the angry screech of cars braking and sirens. Sirens!

We never learnt exactly what happened and we didn't see the faces of our captors until much later. The police broke down our door, burly men with guns, and in that one instant, huddled in front of our TV, we were almost more afraid of them and of the outside. For a teeny, weeny heartbeat, I didn't want to leave the room.

Outside was so bright, our eyes burned, we had to squint. The police half-carried us out and talked to us in a constant stream of soothing platitudes, which I understood by then.' It's all over now.', 'You'll be Ok!', that kind of thing. They were so much bigger and stronger than our captors, I remember thinking giddily, but it's not a fair fight! We didn't hate our kidnappers enough, that was the issue. They had brought us the TV. The policemen (they were all men), were strangers. I couldn't think clearly. In the harsh daylight, Penny's face was creased and the colour of paper. I saw her trying, really struggling to give them the information that they asked for, to answer the constant questions. They asked her more, I guess because she was older, perhaps she looked more sane. In the police car, we were next to each other and given red blankets. I was shaking, I couldn't stop. When my breathing steadied, I looked around. The car was not moving yet. There were other police cars parked all around and officers all around, like ants. We were on a rural lane, I squinted painfully, it hurt to look. Around us were ramshackle white concrete abodes in varying conditions. Some looked relatively smart whilst others were in an advanced state of disrepair. There was a malnourished dog, tethered to a rope. We had heard a dog yelping through the nights and there it was. It, too, needed rescuing. Sombre looking dishevelled people gathered with arms folded in silence and watched. It was a substantial group. The children were barefoot.

It was only later that we learnt what had happened. Someone in the village had dobbed them in, probably hoping for an award. I looked around, incredulous. There it was: this decrepit village, in the middle of the desert, somewhere off the Autopista del Sol, the scene of an impromptu kidnapping. Later, I would question the impromptu nature of it. How had they known that we were there? Was Emma involved in that too? It just didn't seem possible. Some kids just wanting to get rich quick. Looking around, I couldn't really blame them. It didn't work out for them, fortunately for us. I almost felt sorry for them. It was obvious that they had nothing, and for ages I gave them far too much credit for giving us the old TV.

On the drive back to DF, under our festive red blankets, we slept again. In the background of our dreams, the chirrups of the police radio, the guttural voices of the two male officers sitting in the front. They didn't speak to us. Every so often, one would glance at us, I suppose to make sure that we were still breathing. They opened the windows wide, because we stank. We didn't have the energy, then, to be embarrassed about it. After the continuous drone of the highway, we laced through some back streets in Mexico City. They put on their sirens and cut through the traffic like a knife through butter. It seemed so vivid, so tumultuous and over-populated. The open windows let in the teeming roar of urban life, the hot fug of pollution. We had been disappeared for longer than we had thought. We were told that it had been a month. A month! Still swathed in our blankets, we were bundled into the back entrance of the police station and there was a muffled sense of excitement and pride emanating from the officers who had rescued us as they joined their colleagues, lots of chat about 'gringos', some hugs, though not for us.

A kind looking man took DNA swabs and photographs of our faces first of all. Then, individually, we saw a white clad doctor who mercifully spoke English. She was a stern-faced, thin lady, she seemed to want to establish that we were harmed.

"Rape?" she kept asking repeatedly, as if I was lying when I said "No". I was terrified that she would insist on an internal exam to check. Then:

"Beating? Hitting?"

"No!" I repeated again but she raised her plucked eyebrows and looked sceptical. I stood before her in my filthy underwear. I could see her wrinkling her nose. She examined every visible inch carefully, peering into my ears and eyes and then drawing blood. I felt ashamed of the stench that I emitted, of the grime on my skin. Above all, I was horrified at the repulsive odour that I expelled from my mouth.

"You need a dentist." she informed me seriously. As if this would be news to me.

They let us shower in a sterile police shower block. Two cubicles next to each other. It felt alien at first, almost shocking, all those rivulets of warm water cascading over the skin. Dark brown water collected in a pool at my feet. I could hear Penny giggling. The smell of the shower gel was intoxicating, I couldn't get enough of the coconut smell. We rubbed and rubbed at our hair with the shampoo. It was only when our fingers were completely prune-like that we got out and were given the clothes of convicts;

t-shirts and tracksuit bottoms and cheap trainers. We were led back to the doctor, in turn, and she smiled at me for the first time. I had brushed my teeth, even though my gums had bled copiously and obviously I no longer stank.

I was badly malnourished, anaemic and underweight and obviously there would be issues with my teeth but miraculously that was all and I was free to see my dad before the police questioned me further.

"My dad?" I stared at her shocked, "My dad?"

I couldn't believe that he was there and then fury rose in me. I couldn't believe they made me go through all the humiliating medical stuff before seeing him as if I was a criminal! I told them that I had had enough, I didn't stop to consider Penny and how she was alone. I told them they could question me later.

"Wouldn't you rather be clean when he sees you though?" asked the doctor lady with a smile but I ignored her and walked out unimpeded, back to the front desk, opposite which I saw him.

He looked like a shrunken man. He was sitting next to a policeman who looked solid in comparison. My dad was diminished and drawn and haggard, but when he saw me, he leapt to his feet and we hugged. I collapsed into his familiar shape and smell and felt tears course down my cheeks.

"You're alright now." he kept repeating as if reassuring himself.

"They didn't hurt you?"

"No." I confirmed, because they hadn't. The damage had already been done.

Chapter 13

We stayed in Mexico City for one more week, my dad and I. I asked him about my mum, where she was.

"You know where she is." he replied gruffly, "She's overjoyed that you are OK but she wanted me to deal with it, to come and get you."

It had been Elena who had called him, and then immediately after, called the police, on the day following my scheduled return from Acapulco. He had flown out four days later and spent the month stressing in a hotel room, haranguing the Mexican police, who seemed indifferent and dismissive. I missed Elena suddenly.

There was tons of questioning and official police bureaucracy to get through and there was an emergency dentist to visit. A police liaison lady recommended some basic state-funded dentist but my dad insisted on paying for 'the best'. He didn't want me to suffer any more than was absolutely necessary. It wasn't exactly pleasant. I had to have five teeth pulled and a further four filled. The dentist gave me loads of drugs, though, heavy duty drugs. I was basically unconscious through most of it which was a bonus.

We were staying in an anonymous looking hotel, soulless. The type that I had always associated with businessmen, bland and beige. None of the riotous Mexican colour had seeped in. In my mushroom- coloured bed I slept, a lot. We ate in the hotel restaurant which served nondescript food. I felt sad that my dad couldn't experience the exotic Mexican dishes which I knew he'd have loved to try in happier times and chuckle about. He seemed to be afraid of Mexico though. He was afraid of what Mexico had done to me and afraid, consequently, of even venturing outside of the hotel. We didn't speak of my mum but I knew that she was partly to blame for how shrunken he had become, how anxious.

I didn't have to stay for the trial. I was a foreign national and had been traumatised enough. I would be able to give evidence via video link which was a massive relief.

Penny came to see me on the third day. On the interminable journey in the police car back to Mexico City, we had discussed whether we should say anything about Emma, Ed and Enrique. I saw no reason why they should get away lightly but Penny was adamant that No, we mustn't give them up, not for their sakes, but for hers. She had to live and work here, in the same school as Emma! There was no 'going home' for her. I blanched when I thought of the staffroom, of their cold, tight expressions. How Penny would rattle around it alone, diminished, under their scrutiny. She reiterated this rationale when she came to see me. "Really?" I asked her. "How can you stand it, being anywhere near them?"

My dad gave us space and left the room. I was astonished how overjoyed I was to see her. We had been together for so long, albeit involuntarily, that she almost felt like a part of me. She looked clean. It was strange the things that I now noticed! There was colour in her face and we hugged for a long time. Her hair smelt fresh, of coconut shampoo. I was very appreciative now, of pleasant odours. Of course, we had both lost a vast amount of weight. I was skin and bone whereas she was now fashionably slim. She seemed proud of her new physique, sporting tight jeans and a fitted top. I had never seen her wear that particular style before, she was always given to loose-flowing, hippy-type garments.

Penny told me that she had spoken to Stefan and that he had been surprisingly kind. Strangely compassionate, in fact. He had told her, in a perplexed voice, that both Emma and Ed had left from one day to the next and that the school was very short staffed. He wanted her back as soon as possible and also, could you find a way of talking me into staying! I burst out laughing. I couldn't wait to leave, although weirdly, I would miss the job. Not just because of Penny but because I had been good at it. In spite of my looks, not because of, for a change. I wasn't good at much, truth be told. We saw each other every day before my dad and I left Mexico. We even managed to drag my dad out to the bars and restaurants of Coyoacan and he relaxed a bit. I saw him try to summon up the appropriate enthusiasm, but really, his heart wasn't in it. He would laugh sometimes when we forced him to try something particularly spicy. That was lovely to see.

One day, a Saturday, dad and I went to see Elena and to collect my stuff. She gave me a massive hug and there were tears in her eyes. She was very sweet, the distress she had suffered evident on her face. She had been "so, so worried", she kept repeating "so, so worried" and she told me, wringing her hands together, that she knew that I shouldn't have gone, she had always had a bad feeling about it. The irony of it was that, deep down, very deep down, I had always had a bad feeling about that trip too, only I had ignored it. My dad thanked her profusely for calling him. We stayed for tea and cakes, beautifully presented. We sat in the unused living room, like royal guests. My former room looked foreign to me, like a stage set or a scene from a dream. I couldn't remember what it had felt like to inhabit that room. Brad's old hoody was still draped across the bed like evidence from a crime scene, I left it there.

The day before we left Mexico, dad and I had a final hot chocolate with Penny, in a fancy café to say goodbye. Dad would never have let me go alone in any case. He saw his role now as my bodyguard in Mexico. He didn't trust it. I felt a pain in my chest saying goodbye to Penny. I had never had many friends and I knew that she was the real deal. We had literally, physically, supported each other. All my other friends had been wisps, completely insubstantial. Nothing or worse than nothing, much worse.

I gave her a big hug and felt tears blur down my cheeks as I walked away. Dad put his arm around me and gave me a tight squeeze. We returned to the hotel to pack. We walked along a road that crossed one of the ubiquitous highways. The sun was setting. A haze of pink pollution sank over the dirty concrete buildings. I felt a pang of something, not nostalgia but nearly, also fear. Somewhere in this teeming metropolis were my enemies.

As the plane took off into a bright blue sky, I wondered how long Emma would stay in Mexico, whether she felt any remorse. I wondered when she had found out what had happened to us, she must have done, it had been in all the papers. She must have also known that it was their fault, all, ultimately, down to them. I remembered her face, cold and closed, and Enrique's eyes in the mirror, greedy. In my memory or in my imagination, I could no longer tell, his eyes were those of a shark.

Chapter 14

The plane landed in the drizzle at Heathrow as it always does and my fatless body tensed at the insidious onslaught of damp cold. We took a black cab home and trawled through the bleak, colourless suburbs. The air, however, felt fresh and clean. It felt easier to breathe. The driver was a jovial man and obviously wanted a nice chat but my dad and I permeated a solemn silence and he clicked his teeth in disappointment.

At home, my brother had the door open whilst we were still unloading the stuff from the taxi. He looked both familiar and utterly different. He had stretched out in that gawky adolescent boy way and I was surprised when he gave me a hug.

"Wow you look old!" he stared, transfixed, at my face.

His own nose was massive and disproportionate. It looked like the nose of a stranger had landed on his face by mistake.

Our house seemed cramped and drab. My bags took up half of the living room. I didn't remember it being that small.

"Where's mum?" I asked and my brother looked to the floor.

"She's coming later for tea."

"Tea meal or tea drink?" I asked, I don't know why. What did it matter, after all.

"Tea drink, I think" He shuffled off and I remembered to go easy on him. He'd been living through the implosion of our little family alone and trying to cope with adolescence at the same time, as well as the absurd drama of my kidnapping.

In fact, he seemed to have entirely lost his playful, jokey edge. The sarcastic retort, which I had been so used to, was notably absent.

We had been fed so often in the plane that my stomach was a round bloated ball. I hadn't yet become used to normal amounts of food. I made myself a coffee, instead, in the Mexican way. I retrieved a jar of cinnamon from my backpack. The scent filled the kitchen with nostalgia and I wondered how it was possible to miss places where you had been miserable and worse than miserable.

I curled up on the sofa, under a fluffy white blanket, whilst my dad and brother organised things around me as if I was an invalid. They unpacked my bags, processed things through the washing machine, lined everything else up neatly in my room. In a confused hurry, in Elena's flat, we had packed by mistake, a selection of Charles Dickens books from the DF library which I had been meaning to return for about four months. They sat in front of me accusingly with their little luminous official stickers.

At some point I must have fallen asleep, because when I opened my eyes again my mum was sitting in the armchair opposite the sofa, watching me. She looked younger. Her hair had grown. She had always worn it short and practical with a few discreet highlights, now it was far blonder and more vivid and she was wearing a lot of make-up. 'Glamorous' had never been an adjective to apply to my mum in her previous incarnation but that is what she was now, definitely glamorous. She looked sophisticated too, I almost felt proud. Her clothes were smart but understated and fitted her well. No longer the shapeless blue jumpers and leggings of yesteryear, the clothes that she was sporting now screamed 'tailoring!'

Bleary from jet lag and dopey from my nap, I just stared at her confused.

She looked more than concerned, she looked aghast.

"Darling, but you look dreadful!"

"A month locked in a room will do that." I responded drily

"We need to feed you up, have you seen a doctor?"

"'We'? I understood that you no longer live here?"

"Of course, I am here for you! Whatever you need!"

She actually looked distraught to her credit, her eyes wide and tearful. Her mascara was smudging at the corners. I noted that the make-up she wore was expensive. It looked smooth and dewy.

"But from a distance, right?" I wasn't going to let her get away with it easily.

"I didn't mean for any of this to happen." She tried to hang her head, to look ashamed, but there was an edge of defiance about it.

"So why did it happen? Why did you let it?"

"You'll understand one day."

"Don't fucking patronise me! I'm not a kid anymore! You've got no idea what I've been through!"

"So, tell me, Abby, I want to know. Really!" I was sure she did want to know, she had never been heartless, I knew, not to us. She leant forward and put her hand (manicured nails) onto my knee. I was sitting up. The blanket, like a heavy shawl, weighing on my shoulders.

I jerked away.

"What's with the makeover anyway? Is this all for what's-his-face?"

She flinched. The spectre of the Other Man had entered the room.

"His name is Jack." She said quietly, "Maybe you could meet him someday."

I snorted. "That is not going to happen." I thought of my poor crumpled dad.

She got up abruptly and I almost felt bereft. I thought, in that instant, 'that man is more important than me' and it was a clear luminous thought.

"Oh!" she turned round suddenly. Something was remembered.

"Diane called. It was the strangest thing…"

"Diane?" I felt more body grow icy, I drew the blanket tightly around me. Diane was Emma's mum.

Penny and I had never dobbed her in, not to the police and not to my dad. We had agreed. Like all lies, the story had within it the germ of truth. I had told my dad that on the ride back from Acapulco, Penny and I had felt sick and been let out of the car. We were so disorientated that we had wandered off into the desert and got lost. We were unable to find the car again and after searching for us frantically, they must have driven back to Mexico City to get help. There were plenty of holes in this story and had Elena not alerted the police straight away, then no doubt someone would have come around to examining them eventually. As it was, she did so as long as we stuck to our story, they would have gotten away with it unpunished. It made me sick with fury, just thinking about it but I had promised Penny and I couldn't let her down. She was alone in Mexico now.

"What did Diane want?" I tried to sound casual.

"Oh, she wondered if you had seen Emma before you flew back? She said she hadn't heard from her in ages."

Good, I thought, I hope she's dead.

"Er, no, it was so busy, I didn't get a chance."

"Right." I could tell my mum wasn't really buying it.

"Did you two fall out?" she asked coming closer to me, peering at my face.

"No, no, nothing like that. Mum, I'm kind of tired now, I think I need a nap."

I wasn't lying this time.

She left saying that she would be back and I lay back down on the sofa exhausted anew, the harsh sun of the desert burning through my thoughts.

Chapter 15

It was May in the suburbs. The days got longer. Everything was green and flowers were blooming. I had yet to get off the sofa. I lived in my pyjamas. The blanket and I were welded together. Three weeks I had been there. I hadn't planned on this lethargy. It had just happened. Whenever I thought of putting actual clothes on and trying to leave the house, I would feel the most desperate, bone-shattering exhaustion. My dad and my brother would watch me surreptitiously and unhappily but they left me alone. I smelt. I did make myself shower periodically but not very often and obviously not enough. I was fed regularly and copiously a bit like on the long-haul flights. Food appeared at two hourly intervals before me and I ate it whilst staring at the TV like a zombie. I felt a layer of blubber form and coat my stomach. I would watch everything on TV, I was not discerning. I stared as if transfixed, hypnotised.

I became addicted to the soaps, all of them. British, Australian or American, it didn't matter. I followed them obsessively and thought about them obsessively too. The characters lived in my head and my imagination relished their convoluted dramas. I dreamt about their preposterous lives in vivid technicolour. Their voices lulled me to sleep. Soap opera therapy I thought to myself, drily remembering the Mexican soaps garishly broadcast to us in our concrete cell. In many ways I was still there. I had never left.

Twice a week my mum came to visit, always immaculately presented, always alone. She sat opposite me in an armchair and tried to engage me in conversation whilst I shot back snide remarks and stared stubbornly at the TV. She didn't mention Diane or Emma again and I didn't ask. One day, she brought a man. I glared at him in horror and revulsion. How dare she bring Jack into my dad's house? But it turned out not to be Jack and I found it in me to be ashamed of my reaction.

The man was a GP who both of my parents had persuaded (in a combined desperate effort) to look in on me. He looked quite old, up close, but kindly. Obviously not Jack who was, what we used to call, a 'toy boy'. The GP reminded me bizarrely of Enrique's dad, the furrowed brow of the physician, the concern etched on his face or maybe it was just the situation which was the same. Me, still me, unable to escape a sick room.

This man tried to talk to me and I thought that I had better make an effort to respond or they could, they might, put me away somewhere. You heard of such things happening. I could end up jailed in yet another room, not of my choosing. Another bare bulb swinging overhead.

"Physically," he told me "You look pale but relatively healthy. Could you tell me how you are bearing up mentally?"

I decided to tell them what they wanted to hear.

"Initially," I said carefully, "I honestly didn't feel like moving from this sofa but now I am getting stronger every day."

I was glad my family weren't in the room to hear me. It was clearly a load of crap.

The doctor peered at me sceptically, his mouth twisted in a half-smile.

"Yes," I continued brightly "Any day now, I will put on some normal clothes and go back to work."

"Hmmm…" he smiled and patted me on the knee. I heard him afterwards in the hallway, reporting to my dad.

"She's a very smart kid."

He didn't say 'manipulative' but that is what he meant.

"I don't think you need to worry. She will drag herself out of this on her own."

And I did.

Not because of my dad or my brother, whom I felt genuine pity for, but because I got bored.

One morning, I rose from my bed at a decent hour and put on some jeans and a t-shirt. My clothes fitted again. I had put on all the weight that I had lost. The sun was blaring through the window. I encountered my brother in the kitchen and he smiled at me. It was the first genuine smile I had seen from him since I had returned.

"Great! You're up and about!"

"Yes, I thought I might go for a walk."

"A walk?" his brow furrowed, there was a brief pause, "OK I'll come with you."

"Don't think that you have to babysit me!" I felt sorry that his carefree nature seemed to have been squashed under the burden of caring for his quasi-invalid sister.

"No, I'd love to go for a walk!" he enthused.

I sighed. Obviously, it would be a while before I was allowed to go anywhere on my own, but in any event, I was glad of the company.

Immediately, the brightness of the sunlight outdoors hurt my eyes. I felt overwhelmed, disorientated and a bit dizzy. My brother instantly took my arm, as if I was an old lady. I realised then that I had to regain my strength. I couldn't be 19 and decrepit already. We walked to a nearby park. It wasn't far but the muscles in my legs were weak and shaky and when we returned, I had to rest. It had been invigorating to see all the greenery and flowers. I definitely understood that it was good for me. I didn't feel as stale and grey anymore, I felt more open.

We started going on daily walks, my brother and I. I wore sunglasses to make the brightness easier on my eyes. After a few days he no longer took my arm and my muscles no longer shook. I took showers every day. I smelt fragrant again! I started doing normal things as if I meant them. There was a dark patch in my mind which I learnt to conceal. I knew it wouldn't go anywhere but I was determined to keep it under wraps. It was toxic.

A few weeks later, I was striding around the park confidently when, about a hundred metres away on a parallel path, I saw Zoe. The striking yellowish hair was luminous even from a distance. I felt my lungs deflate as if I had been punched in the chest. She had not been there on the highway, of course, but she had been there at the beginning. I felt sure that ultimately, it had been her who had instigated the whole chain of events. I remembered her face as Enrique hugged me in that club, the darkness and envy in it. I turned quickly before she could see me and strode away panting.

Chapter 16

My mum still came over regularly, always for a cup of tea and always for a civilised, albeit superficial, chat. We no longer mentioned Jack. There was never any more talk of me meeting him. Dad and my brother kept out of her way. She would sit next to me in the living room, the blanket there still, my security blanket, and there was warmth in our chat but also it was like talking to a stranger. She looked completely different with her smart, tailored clothes and expensive make-up. Inevitably, she looked younger and not someone who would have kids as big as we were then. She even smelt different. Her signature scent which she had worn for years had been replaced by something prestigious and classy. She had reinvented herself and I didn't really have the energy to fault her for it.

However, my poor dad, who had gone the other way and aged at least ten years, was nowhere near getting over it. In the evenings, he sat in the same armchair drinking. Beer mainly but also vodka sometimes. The TV would be on but his eyes would have a glazed look about them as if he was largely absent. My mother coming to visit me didn't help him. I know deep down that he would have been better off having a clean break from her, but he was a kind man. He thought I needed my mum and he was probably right, but the elegant stranger who visited felt like a mere reflexion of my mum.

One day, she arrived and greeted me tersely. "I feel" she told me, "That we should have a proper chat. You are an adult now, heaven knows that you've been through more than most adults have ever been through and I feel, I feel bad about that…it's terrible timing, because, well because of Jack. But I'd really like you to understand my reasoning, why I have made this decision."

"Because you got bored, I guess." I said coldly

"It's actually a bit more than that!" she bristled. We contemplated each other in silence.

"Are you going to give me a break, or what?" She asked with a nervous laugh.

I sat on the sofa and she sat in the armchair facing me. "OK," I told her, as if I was interviewing her, "Go ahead." She folded and refolded her legs, encased as they were in some shiny looking trousers. They looked incongruous here, in our scruffy sitting room, with evidence of my slovenly presence all around. Biscuit crumbs at that very moment, were sticking uncomfortably to the backs of my thighs. I was wearing shorts made out of a sweatshirt material. I think they were my brother's. I sat cross-legged and contemplated her. She took a deep breath.

"As you know," she began, "Your grandparents were far from well-off."

I pictured my mum's parents then, and sad to say, self-absorbed as I was, they were only a fuzzy blur in my brain

As children, we saw them very rarely, only about once every two years or so. We would drive up to Leeds and spend the day in the over-heated living room of their tiny terraced house. They had one of those fake fires which they placed in a real fire place, which had, as a child, always baffled me, as a concept. They always seemed to me, at the time, extremely old. I was not entirely stupid, I knew that obviously they were old but compared to our dad's mum, who looked and acted vibrant and youthful, they seemed of a different generation entirely. My mum's mum was heavily wrinkled with dark grey hair and a portly appearance. Her dad was also round, albeit taller and was mainly bald with a few strands combed delicately over his scalp. They were both quiet but he, in particular, was virtually monosyllabic. They didn't know how to talk to children and acted around us as if we were adults to whom they were forced to make reluctant polite conversation. We would get sleepy and tetchy round the fire and eventually my mum would put the TV on for us to calm us down. At some point we would be served what my mum's mum referred to as 'a lovely TV dinner,' and when the plates, laden heavily with stew and potatoes appeared, I remember being relieved that the TV was in fact on, and thinking that if it had been off, we wouldn't have been able to eat.

We rarely saw them on big family occasions such as birthdays and Christmas, that's what dad's mum, whom we called Gran, was for. Gran had always had, in my living memory (and still did) vibrant bleach blonde hair and a raucous laugh. Dad's dad had died many years ago when he was a teenager. I had never questioned why we did not see more of my mum's family growing up, why my mum was obviously not closer to them. Knowing how much of a chatterbox on the phone she was, why did I not consider it strange that she never phoned them? She had a brother, who was almost never mentioned, whom we never saw at all. I had had, up until that point, a remarkable lack of curiosity about it all.

"I did not get on with my parents." continued my mum, "Their views were very…limited. They didn't really want much out of life, you know, and I did, that was the difference…"

"Why, what did you want?" I asked, curious in spite of myself, and also baffled. I had never considered my mum to want things in her own right, beyond the needs of the family.

"Well…you'll laugh, it is well…funny thinking about it now, but I was so bored, you know?"

"What?" I repeated impatiently.

"An actress," said my mum, "I wanted to be an actress."

"Oh." I felt even more confused, how had I never known about that?

"I thought, I felt quite strongly…" she continued, "That if only I could somehow get to London, you know, just go to college there and then I could go round the…oh I don't know…the theatres, the actor's agencies or acting schools…it wasn't a coherent plan, you understand, but getting to London seemed to be the most important part of it."

"So, did you? Go to London?"

"No." she sighed heavily, "The only way I could think of to go was to go to University in London, that was the only legitimate route I could think of. Every so often, quite rarely, someone from my area of Leeds would go off to university 'down south' and for the rest of us it would be as if they were going somewhere foreign or exotic. Adults would speak of it with the same mystified reverence as if they were talking about a trip to the moon. For me, specifically, it meant they were escaping all the…all the drabness."

"So why didn't you do that then?"

"After my O-levels, both of my parents sat me down and told me that my lofty ambitions were unrealistic and I needed to get a job and start paying my way. I was devastated. The irony is that I had done well in my O-levels and could easily have, eventually, found my way to university. But that wasn't even the worst of it…"

"Oh no, that's terrible, poor you! What was the worst of it?" This story felt to me, a bit like a soap opera and I found myself revelling in it.

"It was…it still makes me furious thinking about it…it was my brother, he was, well he is, three years older and he had the same stupid lofty ambitions…I mean what are the chances right?" she spat out, her face convoluted and twisted in an old anger.

"Two kids from a poor northern neighbourhood, both with impractical silly ambitions! Both wanting to be actors! Who would have thought that possible?"

I kept quiet. I had an idea what was coming.

She crossed and uncrossed her legs. Agitated she stood up and walked across to the pavement to survey the uneventful suburban street.

"Well, you did make it to London…or to a small town next to it, anyway!" I couldn't resist, but she turned on me, furious.

"My brother, my bloody brother was allowed to go to London to study drama and he made it! He actually sodding made it! He's in theatres, he's on TV, he's even in bloody commercials!"

"Oh wow!" I yelped, "Would I have seen him in anything?"

"That's not the point!" she hissed darkly. "The point is…" she looked at me exasperated, dramatic herself and suddenly, I could picture her as an actress on a stage somewhere, floating about, swinging her head, expressing herself.

"The point is that he got the chance to escape but I never did."

"But you are actually here!"

"Yes," she glared at me frustrated, "But it was too little too late at that point."

She sat back down on the sofa; her shoulders slumped in a sudden exhaustion.

"After the O-levels, I got a job as a junior in an office. The office was in an industrial estate off a motorway. Every morning I would need two buses to get there, it was always raining and cold and…it was the most depressing thing… I would sit in this tiny windowless room, sorting files out, putting these invoices away. I was too sad to even focus. Everyone else there was middle-aged, but they looked old to me of course. All you could hear was their whiny bored voices and the roar of the motorway."

She looked at me and I could picture it clearly and I did feel pity. I tried to imagine a young version of my mum. I had only ever seen a few grainy photos. She was short and had mousy brown hair naturally but she was pretty. Probably not glamourous enough to be an actress at the time, I thought, but I kept that to myself.

"What happened then?"

"Well…another friend from school who also hadn't gone on to do A-levels, well I started hanging around with her, because, the way I saw it, we were in the same boat whilst the others were in a different, better boat."

"We hadn't been friends before." She continued, "Before in school I mean, we were never that alike before."

"Why? What was she like?"

"Oh, nice enough, really pretty, 'a party girl' my mum called her but it wasn't in a complimentary way, if you know what I mean. When people said 'party girl' back then, they basically meant prostitute, give or take. In school, I was always in a different set, she was in the thick set."

"I'm presuming it wasn't called that officially." I laughed

"No," she grinned despite herself, "Officially it was called the Special Class, but teachers would openly talk about the kids in it as being retarded. That's how things were then."

"So, your friend wasn't super bright, I take it."

"She was called Karen. No, I would like to say that she was street smart, but no, not so much that either!"

We were both laughing openly then. It was the most relaxed moment I had shared with my mum for years.

"Well, what did you and Karen get up to?"

"We went to all the local pubs, such as they were…I had a curfew, she didn't, her family were a bit all over the place to be honest. Anyway, I had a curfew so we didn't have the time to go far, into the centre of town I mean, because without a car, back then that was a good trek. And then… at some point, she met this bloke, or perhaps she already knew him, anyway, he had a car and she made him promise to get us home in time for my curfew. All a bit dodgy, but we were determined…to be honest, at that point, I was so miserable, I didn't even care. I would have done anything for kicks. Anyway, I barely remember the bloke, he had side-burns, but he was as good as his word. He would take us to the pubs in the centre of town which were more exciting for us, they had music and dancing, and then drop us back home. Of course, he was pissed driving, but no one cared about that back then. I think, looking back on it, that he must have fancied Karen, or maybe she was doing something for him, otherwise I can't imagine what he would be getting out of the arrangement…"

"OK," I was impatient for the meat of the story, "What happened then?"

"Well," my mum looked suddenly serious, "At one of the pubs in the centre, it had dancing, I recall, I met your dad, he asked me to dance…there you have it, here am I, or rather not anymore as it were."

"What do you mean 'there you have it'! How did you get from a pub in Leeds to a suburb of London?"

My mum sighed and went back to look out of the window. She wasn't laughing anymore her face was sombre.

"So, your dad and I got together, and he's a good bloke, I'm not taking that away from him, I never said different…he said he had a job lined up in London, he actually did, I mean, he wasn't lying about it and I got super excited and basically pestered him to marry me, after only a few months. He was such a patient, kind person, that he agreed. I mean, I had to get out of there! That office with the filing…if I'd had to stay there much longer, I'd have found a way to burn it down!"

"Wow, what did your parents say?"

"Well, obviously, they were really sniffy and suspicious, totally sure that I was pregnant of course…why else would I jump on the first bloke I met? I think that, by then, they had forgotten the whole acting thing, I mean, I never mentioned it in front of them anymore, they probably thought that it was a phase that I had grown out of."

"Were you? Pregnant?" I asked quietly, desperately trying to calculate the dates in my head

"No! Not you too! Of course not, not yet…"

"OK, so in London…did you try, well…acting?" I struggled to picture it in my head, the mum I had grown up with, a very average lady, scurrying about to auditions wearing heavy make-up, standing on stages in front of directors. It was such an unlikely, alien image.

"Yes, yes, of course I tried, for years I tried. There was, there might still be, this newspaper called The Stage where all the auditions were listed and I would go to at least one a day, often more than one, for years, and very rarely, I would get a call-back, but it never went further than that. And there were millions of us, millions of us hopeful, or rather hopeless, actors, and all the girls were taller and prettier than me, and far more glamourous, oh, that was a given…"

She sunk deep into the sofa and put her head back, I could see the ageing in her neck, the little pouch of fat under her chin. From this angle, I thought cruelly, no amount of make-up could help her.

"Your dad was working really hard, but I wasn't, see? I had to be free to go to auditions! He understood that, and he took the brunt of it, but he couldn't support the both of us on his wage, not really, we rented this cramped studio flat and lived like paupers. We ate bread and potatoes and beans, thats all. At some point, he had enough I guess, it was fair enough. There had been about four, five years of it…going nowhere and my bloody brother, all that time, on the stage, in the west end. It actually made me sick…It was the drama school, see? That's what catapulted him! I never had that…I, well… I moved here, we moved out here, it was much cheaper, and had kids and the rest you know. I got a job in an office, always the same kind of job…" she laughed drily, "though, to be fair, it was never as bad as my first job, at least…"

"OK." I was struggling to understand, I felt as if I had missed something, "So, dad was basically kind and accommodating, why would you leave him, then?"

"I never disputed that he was kind and accommodating! Yes, definitely that and more! But I never loved him! He was my ticket to London, no more and no less!"

I stared at her.

She saw my face and paused, a minute of indecision on her face, but then a hardening, a resolution.

"No, I'm sorry, you're old enough now to know the truth…it was like an arranged marriage!" she laughed again, shortly. I had never witnessed her before, so bitter. "Arranged by me to be fair…I would have given anything to be an actress. My brother being a success was like a red flag to a bull, it made me so mad, I would have done anything…"

"And dad happened to be 'anything'" I kept staring at her. I couldn't really process what she was saying. They had never been the most affectionate couple, that was certainly true, but people weren't then…certainly not people from the north. I always thought that was it…and they were really loving to us kids, when I thought about the frigid atmosphere in Zoe's house, we never had anything like that, my brother and I.

I did feel for her a small worm of pity. If it hadn't been for the devastation that she had visited upon my dad, it would have been a much bigger worm.

"Let me guess," she looked up at me, her head had been down, contemplating the cheap carpet, "You met someone that you finally had feelings for, us kids big enough to deal with it, you thought, sod it."

"I wouldn't have put it like that exactly."

"But that's the gist, isn't it?"

"Well yes, but not 'sod it,' of course, I care about your dad, of course, I don't want to see his little pouchy ruined face every time I come here…but I have strong feelings for Jack, it is true. Feelings, which I have never felt before. It may be love or not, I am too old to deal in cliches…"

"And yet you are! Dealing in a cliché! Actually, living one!" She looked at me, trying to figure out how mean I was being. I could tell by her face, that I had become a stranger to her, that she could no longer read me.

"OK, I can see you're upset," she told me, "We can talk about it again another time."

She looked haggard and drained as she left and I sat on the sofa, cross-legged, mulling it over.

My brother, halfway through his A-levels, was also far more mature than he should have been. There was a seriousness about him. Not studiousness, neither of us had ever been particularly studious, it was mainly an absence of fun and mischievousness, which had been one of his defining characteristics. As far as I knew, he didn't know the whole backstory to the mum and dad saga and I didn't want to burden him with it, at least not yet.

It was Simon, more than my dad, who took over the day to day running of the house which had been the domain of my mum. All those petty, thankless tasks without which things start looking disgusting. My dad, at home, had this kind of lumbering, hopeless look about him, as if he was never quite sure what was going on. As I got stronger, I helped Simon around the house.

When I thought that I felt completely 'normal' again, I went back to the restaurant I had worked at before. I was part-time initially for selfish reasons. I wanted to have it easy. I told the manager what I had been through but I didn't tell the rest of the staff, the vast majority of whom, in any case, were new there. New to me anyway. They had joined whilst I was in Mexico. They seemed to have moved en-masse from another restaurant. They weren't gap year kids. They were older, in their twenties, a tougher, harder bunch. But that didn't bother me. The most intimidating thing for me, initially, was that they all knew each other really well.

It quickly became apparent that I shouldn't have said anything to the manager at all, as the others resented me getting out of things, as they saw it. Being let off the more hardcore cleaning, for instance. I heard them whispering and chuckling and guessed it was because they thought that the manager fancied me. He didn't notice because he was hidden in his office most of the time but I felt painfully self-conscious.

Most shocking of all, was that Paul was working there parttime as a kitchen porter. Whenever I saw that shock of bright yellow hair bent over the industrial sized sink, I felt a chill run through me even though it was always boiling in the kitchen. It was fortunate for me that he was always stuck there by the sink because I didn't want to talk to him. I could barely manage the most basic of greetings, the words would stick in my throat. I'd feel him staring whenever he could with that bland moon face. Staring as if he wanted to bleed me dry.

Time passed and I got into a routine. The days got longer and warmer. I started behaving as if I was normal. I worked more shifts. I no longer avoided the more tedious tasks and I was accepted by my

colleagues, slowly at first, but before long I was gossiping alongside them and staying for lock-ins, drinking whiskey out of tumblers. Fortunately, Paul never got involved in any extra-curricular drinking, he had to go straight home.

Physically and mentally, I became harder and sharper. I tried not to think. I tried not to feel. After a while it became easier, like a habit. I smoked and I drank most nights and I started to hang out with my colleagues outside work as well. There were two boys and two girls. All of them, except one boy, Tom, lived on the same estate near to the restaurant. It was a shoddy, downtrodden estate perched incongruously near to the fancy road which our restaurant was on. The two girls, Trish and Beck, somewhere in their mid-twenties, shared a one-bedroom flat. Both 'boys,' also men in their mid-twenties, shared a flat with their single mums. However, the one who resided on the estate, Ben, always had the flat to himself. His mum mysteriously 'worked nights' and that was where most of the debauchery occurred. Like the others, I was soon spending all my wages on drugs. Mainly weed, the odd 'E'. Why not? I thought. It's not as if I was saving to travel, look how that had panned out.

It was hot summer by then. The flat had a concrete balcony and we would sit on metal chairs, smoking whatever we had, giggly, our feet up on the railings, the heat ricocheting from hard surface to hard surface and bouncing back to us. Our skin burned. There was a sour taste, always in my mouth.

My mum still came to see me and I did feel a new understanding there, a better tolerance, but at the end of the day, I still felt a huge pity for my dad and I was incredibly self-absorbed. Feelings for other people didn't settle on me, really, for long. I was proud of myself. I seemed to have recovered from my ordeal. I was actually making friends. I wasn't sure what these people were to me though. A mutual convenience of sorts, perhaps. My mum looked worried however. A frown hovered over her perfectly made- up face and before long my dad was kindly and subtly interrogating me about my new friends. He suggested that they may be a bad influence, I smothered a snort of derision. The 'bad influence' was already in my head.

It was midsummer in London when we were summoned to the police station for me to testify at the trial of the would-be kidnappers by video link. I dressed smartly and I slicked my hair back into a bun. I wore more makeup than usual. The police station was very modern as if it had just been newly decorated and the policeman, young and gawky, who had been tasked with accompanying me, couldn't stop staring at me. I still got that sometimes, though not quite as much as before. I think people were put off by my newly acquired hard edge. We sat in a pristine room surrounded by screens and a microphone and a lady technician came to attach another small mic to my top. On one of the screens, I saw myself and I was shocked. I barely looked at myself any more. I looked like a grim, serious person. A humourless person, a stranger.

We waited for some time in an awkward silence and then the screen opened up before us and there was a courtroom with a high ceiling in an ornate, old-fashioned building. It looked like a drama on TV and I forgot, briefly, that they could see me. I was staring at the defendants. They looked so young, like kids, younger and far skinnier than my brother. They weren't younger, of course, but they were so malnourished that I guessed that they had never grown. I couldn't believe that these kids, kids whom I could have squashed, right then, in the palm of my hand like flies, could have had the gumption and the wherewithal to hold us captive for a month.

There was a translator who spoke loudly, shockingly loudly, into my earpiece. I was required, primarily, to identify them. I had seen their faces after we'd been rescued but even if that had not been the case, I would have recognised them. I knew their eyes. Dark, unfathomable and hungry. I recalled vividly, in that instant, the smell. The smell of their rancid clothes, of our stinking cell, of our own fetid skin. I even remembered the aroma of the food which we were always starving for.

The translators voice in my ear asked if they had beaten me? No. Raped me? No.

The boys had their heads down. They were wearing grey jumpsuits and their hands were cuffed in front of them. The cuffs looked enormous on their skinny wrists. I felt a twinge of pity.

I looked around the courtroom on the screen and started, almost jolted, out of my seat so that the policeman leaned forward to steady me and put one large paw on my shoulder as if in comfort. I started because I had seen Penny, although I have no idea why I was surprised, of course she'd be there. She had told me on numerous occasions that she would stay in DF, that she had nowhere else to go. She was sitting silently in a witness box next to a smooth, smartly dressed lady who reminded me of Elena, all make-up and business suit. Clearly, that was her lawyer. What really saddened me though was that Penny did not look well. She had put on weight again, but that was not it. She looked puffy and pale and bloated and her happy mouth was sagging downwards. I wanted to crawl through the screen and go to her and hug her. We could see each other. I knew that the whole courtroom could see me, but I never saw her turn my way and I felt bereft. I didn't see her testify. I had said my piece and my screen was switched off. Later I would find out that they had been sentenced to 15 years each. The staring policeman accompanied me to the front desk and then that was that. I walked emptily into the summer afternoon feeling a gnawing sensation in my mind as if something was upsetting me that I couldn't fix. I wasn't working that day so I went straight to Ben's to get stoned.

Chapter 17

I rarely went to Ben's on my own. There was usually at least one other person present, we were pack animals after all. I didn't even know if he'd be there, he could well have been working. Obviously, we all worked different shifts. He opened the door to me though. He looked dopey and disoriented as if I had woken him although it was three in the afternoon by then. He was wearing a grimy t-shirt and tracksuit bottoms and his eyes were puffy. Behind him, I glimpsed a female figure in a pink towelling robe, the mysterious mum, and when she turned to me, I jolted. She looked haggard and old, much more worn out than she should have been. So, this is what happens, I thought. She seemed to be missing a tooth but when she caught me staring, she quickly clamped a hand over her mouth.

"Well, aren't you a pretty one!" she exclaimed in a mock friendly voice but her eyes were hard blue pebbles.

"Leave it mum!" mumbled Ben and then to me; "Do you want to come in?"

I didn't really then. I suddenly didn't know what the hell I was doing there, standing in that doorway with those strangers. In my head I heard the screeching hum of the Mexican highway, the anonymous voices shouting for me.

"Come on!" Ben grinned at me in his familiar sleepy way and poked me in the midriff. I was still dressed in my ridiculous smart clothes. I saw his mum retreating into her room.

"You're here now." he said.

I followed him into his room which smelt familiar to me, musty and slightly damp. We always went there to smoke. He reignited the joint which was half-smoked on his bedside table and we sat on his unmade bed with our backs against the wall. My heartbeat slowed. I felt my muscles relax. He put on some music and we sat for some time in silence.

Where have you been then, all dressed up?" he looked me quizzically up and down.

Of course, he had never seen me look smart outside of work. I told him about the court case, a no-frills version and he just stared at me.

"I can't believe you went through all that! Fuck."

He just kept staring and then a thought clouded his eyes.

"Are you.er...Ok? Did they do stuff to you?"

Ben was pale and thin. He had dark blue eyes and brown hair. I had never thought of him as a boy before. It had never entered my mind, but in that instant, I really wanted to kiss him, maybe more. Something. I wanted something.

"No," I replied softly "they didn't do anything to me."

I leant in then and kissed him. He opened his eyes wide in shock but then he complied. He tasted sour. He tasted of tobacco and weed and under it the vague tang of minty toothpaste.

Soon we were rolling around on his unmade bed. I wanted to escape my memories. Penny's face on the monitor. What it had felt like to be parched for days. The way that loneliness had solidified over me like iron and what I had become. I needed to forget that most of all.

Afterwards, we smoked a normal cigarette on the balcony and the sky was turning orange and pink and it was still warm. My hair was spread loose over my shoulders and behind us Ben's mum wafted about in her robe.

Ben and I became boyfriend and girlfriend but not in a traditional sense. We would never have called each other that, those particular names. However, whenever we were not at work at any time of day or night, we were together in his flat.

His mum never said much. I got the impression that she didn't like me.

"Sure, she does," shrugged Ben "She's just kind of jealous."

"Jealous?" I was baffled. How could a grown woman, a mum, be jealous of me?

"Because you're so pretty!" said Ben, who didn't seem confused by it. It seemed weird to me. To be jealous of a woman who you're not even competing against.

Someone who was definitely jealous was Paul. He would glare at me every time that I went into the kitchen, his bright fringe plastered onto his forehead with sweat, his eyes round with greed and rage. He wanted to be included in our gang. He wanted to be near me. Then, to add insult to injury, he witnessed me and Ben playfighting once in the doorway of the kitchen. Even though, as a couple, we were very non-touchy in public, I guess Paul picked up on something and his eyes narrowed and from then on, he wouldn't even look at me. The rest of the 'gang' found me and Ben funny, hilarious even. Trish told me that they'd never seen Ben with a girl and they had known him for years. They had presumed that he was gay. I had realised, belatedly, that Trish and Beck were gay. They weren't physical around each other either but once I had caught a glimpse of them kissing. Nobody ever remarked on it though. I guess with them, and now with me and Ben, the priority was never sex, but drugs.

The drugs ran deeper with them than I had realised. Now that I was around Ben's all the time, I saw that it was much more than weed and the odd 'E', my default justification. No, it was also coke and speed and one day I walked in on them all smoking something that smelt harsher, more toxic, than usual.

"What is that?" I asked innocently.

"Just a different type of weed." replied Tom, slurring a bit. They all looked collectively cagey though.

That night, when we were alone, I interrogated Ben about it. It was clear that he didn't want to tell me, but eventually he admitted that it was heroin and it wasn't the first time. Then he looked sheepish and added that they avoided smoking it in front of me as they saw me as a bit naïve.

"Naïve!" I yelped and punched him on the arm. Half joking but really quite offended.

"Yes, well. You're going off to Uni. You're a college kid. We're just, you know, we're just different."

I had always known that they had no real ambitions but I'd never really thought about it. It had always been irrelevant. I never thought about going to University. In fact, I had almost forgotten about it. Right then, I felt like another person entirely. I felt more like one of them. A kind of lost boy. As if I was wearing a mask, a disguise which I had inadvertently grown into. Ben had left school after GCSEs and gone to a sixth form college to do a BTEC in design technology. Then, he'd started working in restaurants full-time and never looked back.

"Don't you want to do anything else?" I asked him, tentatively. I didn't want to imply that his life was pointless.

"Yup, maybe one day." he mumbled skinning up and I realised in that instant, that this could be me too. That this was exactly what my parents were afraid of. This. Drifting forever in a dead-end job, permanently stoned with no plans and no decent income. They had only stopped nagging because it was August and I was due to start university in September.

Chapter 18

Penbridge was considered to be a beautiful, historic university which had fallen on hard times in recent years, very likely through mis-management. Consequently, it was no longer considered elite and accepted normal, average students. Basically, kids like me, who wanted the university experience but weren't considered brilliant. I knew all this because our Head of Sixth form had believed in telling kids the absolute truth. Hence, why I applied there and, notwithstanding the prettiness factor, why I got in. In the interim, of course, and with all that had happened, I had almost forgotten all about it. I could barely remember the person who I had been when I had gone to the interview. I looked back on that silly creature with a kind of bitter nostalgia.

In early August, I received literature about accommodation and I poured over it obsessively. I was firmly cemented to Ben at that time and all I thought about was securing privacy for us for when he visited. Of course, I didn't tell my parents this. I explained to them that I felt older because of 'everything that I had been through', which was actually true, and therefore didn't want to live in close proximity with a multitude of other students. They fell for it, of course. I picked an expensive flat share with only three others and a large study bedroom just for me. They were so happy that I was going to university, that they would have agreed to anything.

In recent months, since I'd been hanging out with the 'gang at work' as they referred to it, my mum and dad had been meeting up to talk about me. I could tell that my dad was pathetically hopeful about these meetings. In his fantasies, I think, he imagined that they would eventually lead to my mum's return. It made me so cross, at both of them.

"Seriously dad," I scowled at him, "She left you for another bloke, why would you want her back?"

I told my mum that she should just spell it out for him in black and white, tell him the story which she had told me; that it would stop him hoping at least.

"He always knew my real motives, more or less." is what she told me.

"More or less is not good enough, you really need to make it super clear!"

Ironically, I was getting on better with my mum. Even when she got on my case, I secretly admired how strong-willed and opinionated she'd become. Also, how stylish she now was. Superficial as I was, that was probably what I admired the most. I hadn't seen much of my brother that summer. He'd been working in a bakery on the high street. In the evenings, he'd come home with half-stale iced buns, doughnuts and hard white bread, his skin speckled with flour. He had a yeasty smell.

"I'll miss you when you leave." he told me seriously one evening, as we sat at the kitchen table picking at bits of broken gingerbread men which he'd brought home. I raised an eyebrow at him, expecting him to smirk and say "Only joking!" as he would have done in the past, but he didn't. He only looked sad and worried and fiddled with some crumbs.

September came and the cool winds arrived.

My dad drove me to Penbridge. I had bid goodbye to my mum the previous afternoon. I could sense the relief from both my parents radiating off them in waves. Mainly, relief that I would be a long way away from Ben and the 'gang'. Also, that my life was now, once again, following a trajectory which was considered normal, something acceptable. I had received a hurried, self-conscious hug from my brother as he left the house that morning.

"Keep well." he mumbled, a bit grimly and we both recalled the last time that I had gone anywhere.

I had seen Ben and the others the previous night. They had all been a bit dismissive, I thought. Another college kid who was abandoning them, but Ben, in the candlelight of his room when we were alone, looked downcast.

"I wish that you weren't leaving." he said quietly and I was surprised. I suppose that I hadn't realised that his feelings ran that deep. He always seemed so flippant about his own life, so indifferent. It was me that cared less in that instant, who was suddenly bored of it all: getting stoned, the semi-sarcastic posturing, dealing with stroppy customers, the grey soulless concrete of the estate, the constant drug-induced fatigue.

Suddenly, I wanted to be somewhere new.

On that interminable journey up the motorway to the North West, I left the window open and the cool breeze cleaned the last vestiges of weed from my brain. No longer befuddled, I felt clear and pure and excited for the first time in months, if not years.

The driveway of the central compound of Penbridge and the imposing edifice itself looked like something out of a period drama. Ancient birch trees lined up on either side of a beautiful lane which led to a magnificent circular driveway with an elaborate fountain in its centre. That was where students were deposited whilst the parents were directed to somewhere less picturesque to park. Registration took place in the main building in what would have been, at some stage, a ballroom. The dimensions of the space were intimidating. I saw clearly, in that second, us all scurrying beneath those high, high ceilings, as inconsequential as ants. There were intricate mouldings on the ceilings and walls but up close, as I peered carefully, they looked dusty and chipped and neglected. To the rear of the main building, I glimpsed the entrance to the library, widely displayed in all the literature. I guessed that this too would be exceptionally grand.

The other kids looked young to me, giggly and sweet of face. My dad was very upbeat standing in the queue next to me, looking round with his eyes wide open,

"Well Abs, this is fancy, isn't it!"

I didn't want to burst his bubble. I tried to keep my cynicism in check. I wanted to say, but didn't: 'This is all a front'. I was right. Once we had completed registration and security and numerous other bits of paperwork, we were led in groups to our designated accommodation and even my dad looked dejected then. Behind the ornate façade of the main building were concrete blocks lined up in rows and reminiscent of Ben's estate. These blocks housed the various accommodation options but also the different faculties. We were given little maps. The humanities building was located at quite a distance from the main building and close to a wood, shown on the diagram as a few stick trees but in actuality, dark and dense.

 The whole campus was extremely rural and gave the impression of being quite wild. Concrete blocks notwithstanding, that was the truly beautiful aspect of it. Overgrown paths led through dense thickets and trailed through shady woods heavy with massive fir trees. Small creatures could be heard rustling through the foliage and even the mass of chattering teens quietened in awe, their eyes widening in surprise. The brochures did not do this place justice. Perhaps they'd forgotten that it was like this or maybe they'd applied to university late and blindly. I had never seen it before but I loved it; the low hanging clouds, the green bucolic vistas, the rawness of the wind. My dad looked a bit doubtful.

"I hope that this is well-lit at night. I can't see many lamp posts, can you?"

It was still daylight but he was right. It was a place of shadows and hidden corners.

My accommodation, my flat, was located on the ground floor of Block C. Of course, what I hadn't thought through carefully enough was the rationale behind other people also requesting remote accommodation, away from the blustering stream of humanity. Obviously, my flatmates were weirdos, at the best misfits. That was immediately apparent.

There was Julian, an obese lumbering musician. Carrie, a twitchy exchange student from Idaho and DeeDee whom I warmed to almost at once. She had dyed pink hair and eyebrows painted on so that they looked excessively arched. She was sitting at the kitchen table in our 'communal area' rolling a cigarette but I could easily picture her skinning up. She looked just the type, scrappy and a bit mean.

"Well," she nodded drily to me and my dad.

"This is a view, isn't it?" She gestured behind her to where a wide low window displayed the rubbish and recycling area for the whole of Block C., I chuckled but my dad looked horrified.

"Oh no, Abs, shall we see if we can move you?"

"Don't worry dad, I'll be fine." I sat down next to DeeDee and grinned, took out my cigarettes.

My dad studied me, frowning.

"Will I be off then love? Will you be OK?"

I saw him out and gave him a hug. I hoped he would find some other excuse to keep seeing mum, for his sake.

Chapter 19

As soon as my dad had left, Deedee and I started on a bottle of wine which she'd brought with her. She'd had it chilling in the fridge. We sat next to each other at the kitchen table, smoking. She had taken a gap year as well but had had the traditional positive experience; India, Thailand and Australia, the normal backpacker route. Deedee was bubbly with a flip side, that was my initial impression. I didn't tell her anything at first. I had actually planned not to say anything to anyone here about my gap year experiences. Halfway through our bottle of wine, Julian came in and leant against the fridge looking at us. He seemed worn and crumpled in his clothes. His brown hair was cropped close to his head and he had a double chin and some spots around his mouth which was oddly red and moist and partially open.

Deedee grinned at him and gestured widely;

"Hey! Join us! Get a glass!"

He picked a tumbler from the neatly arranged glasses and plates in the kitchen cabinets and tentatively pulled up a chair. Once there, he didn't have much to say but sat there looking nervous, almost cagey.

Deedee ploughed on though, interrogating him. She seemed to possess an uncontrollable exuberance and desire for information. She would have made a great detective, that's what I used to think. Falteringly, Julian revealed that he was from the Midlands and here to study Music.

"Music?" questioned Deedee in a loud, puzzled voice, "Is that a thing?"

"Obviously, it's a thing, it's what Julian is studying." I rescued him while he gaped fish-like. He smiled at me gratefully. Maybe he decided in that moment to be loyal to me, I don't know. After a few glasses of wine, he relaxed too and then Deedee went to get the emergency vodka that she had hidden in her room. We stared at her.

"Are you just a walking off-license?!" I laughed,

She raised her elaborate eyebrows at me.

"I figured it would be too late for us to venture out into the countryside," she gestured through the windows, where the bins stood in gloomy shadows, "until tomorrow, in search of booze."

The vodka was the cheap kind, with the indecipherable foreign label. We were just getting started on it and getting used to the acidic, toxic tang of it, when Carrie came in. We knew that she was American but she didn't really look it. For instance, she had really bad teeth. Our knowledge of Americans came mostly from films and she certainly didn't have the wholesome look that we were used to seeing on screen. I had seen gringos in Mexico of course, had worked with them, but they seemed of a different species entirely too, oddballs who couldn't hack life in the states for whatever reason.

 Carrie was pale and petite with blotchy skin and hair dyed an unfortunate garish yellow. I presume it was supposed to be blonde. It reminded me of Zoe and Paul and for one second, I felt a chill. Goosebumps rose along my arm. But she wasn't lumpen as they were, she was as tiny as a child and on the kitchen chair, she folded in on herself to look even smaller. She told us that she was on a scholarship here to study medicine. She spoke in a surprisingly low, faltering voice and we all took a moment to take stock and try to picture her clad in a white coat in a hospital setting. It was impossible to do. A more incongruous candidate would be difficult to imagine.

We started to relax with each other then, vodka loosening our tongues and revealing, in my new flatmates, varying degrees of sharpness and cynicism. We were all misfits, for obvious reasons, even though I had given myself that status in my head. I didn't know what others saw. I presumed it was not good. None of us minded though. What I mean is, we weren't sheepish or embarrassed about being different from the masses. Even at this tender age, we were all nineteen, we had embraced our weirdness fully already.

Julian had taken a year off after his A-levels, but not to travel anywhere or even to work. He was initially reluctant to divulge anything, but finally admitted to having had 'some issues to work through'. We stopped questioning him then.

Carrie had not taken a break in her studies. The American system was a bit different. She had been put forward by a special committee which granted exceptional 'honours' student scholarships to study abroad.

"Why did you choose Penbridge?" asked Deedee, her mad eyebrows slanted.

"I looked at a map. It was remote."

That's all she said and then looked down, pulling her sweatshirt over her fingers. Even the tumbler with the vodka looked incongruous with her clutching it. She looked like a child doing something inappropriate.

"We need snacks!" cried Deedee sometime later and went to retrieve various bags of crisps from her room. We all laughed and then Julian appeared with a packet of supermarket doughnuts with white frosting. We hadn't eaten anything that evening, so that became dinner. The icing was saccharine against our teeth, our sticky fingers left blurry marks on the cheap tumblers.

Later still, drunk, we all returned to our individual rooms. We all had our own ensuite bathroom, the shower over the toilet. It reminded me of Emma's studio flat in Mexico, I felt a residual reminder of my sickness when I had stayed there. The vodka and the sugary doughnuts churned about in my stomach. I put my uncovered duvet and pillowcase onto my single bed. The mattress was covered with a plastic sheet. Ignoring all the suitcases and bags, I fell onto the bed and passed out.

Chapter 20

The next day dawned grey and windy. We wandered around the kitchen, making instant coffee, which all of us seemed to have brought from home. We were all much less sparkly, unsurprisingly, dull in fact. We tried to avoid the sight of the refuse through the rain-soaked windows. The smell, however, seeped through, and we started to learn to breathe through our mouths. We didn't realise yet, but the odour would worsen as time went on. That morning, we were jittery, hungover and confused. We all had to enrol in our various faculties and sort out our timetables. For the most part, we hadn't even unpacked. A piled ashtray still sat on the kitchen table. We all avoided it.

The wind was bitter here. It felt like another country, remote and Nordic. The heavy trees shuffled, swayed and glistened in the continuous drizzle. I set off with other people from my accommodation block down the winding path that led to the humanities block. I was glad that I wasn't alone. The distances were vast and I walked briskly into the astonishing cold. Twenty minutes later, I arrived at another concrete block. It was a different shape to the accommodation one but it was constructed with the same grim dark stone. There was a sign over the door which identified it as the humanities faculty and inside there was a reception desk such as you would find in any soulless office. The famed prettiness of Penbridge clearly did not extend this far.

We were all herded into an uninspiring classroom with a flickering overhead neon light. In spite of the early hour, the building was in darkness. It was surrounded by the ubiquitous, massive fir trees and barely any light entered. The room was full of fresh-faced students. The ones who were like me but somehow much younger and not just by a year. It was in their eyes, a guilelessness.

The Head of the English department was a serious lady called Sylvia. She gave a presentation and introduced us to various members of the faculty. They all seemed quite conservative and staid, all more or less middle-aged except for two youngish men. One was clad in sports gear from head to foot. He wore shorts and that baffled me, how was he not cold? He immediately explained that he coached rugby if anyone was interested. This announcement was met with giggling for some reason. I didn't find it either funny or interesting myself. In fact, I immediately forgot his name. The other youngish man looked clever. If he were American, he would be called 'preppy', but he was a Brit. A posh Brit, bespectacled and well-spoken. As he spoke, the rain started battering the glass in the windows and we all looked round startled. The Head of English chuckled from the side of the room, as if it was a delightful joke.

"You'll have to get used to the weather here kids, it's not great!"

"Worst weather in the country!" agreed the preppy man grinning. He had introduced himself as James. I thought of him as a gringo though. The windows didn't look strong enough to withstand the onslaught. I stared at them transfixed. Through the smears of rain, I was sure that I saw movement in the thicket of trees. A brown shape, some kind of animal, I thought, bigger than a dog, I tensed. I stared and stared but then I had to blink and when I checked again it had disappeared.

We were given individual timetables. All of us studying straight English had an identical syllabus, the only variable was the identity and scheduling of the tutor. The first thing I noticed was that the timetable was not too onerous. I had just three hours of lectures per day.

"Lots of time for reading!" Sylvia explained, peering at us earnestly.

There followed a long dull talk about the library and how it worked. I stared out of the windows but there was just trees and dense foliage, the rain obliterated everything. The cacophony of it nearly drowned out Sylvia's speech, she raised her voice until she was nearly shouting. I peered down again at my timetable and noticed that my tutor was James. I glanced at him surreptitiously. He was standing to the side again, pretending to listen to Silvia. His long slim fingers were drumming against the sides of his dark wool trousers. He was dressed smarter than everyone else there. He must have felt me staring because he glanced at me quickly and I shivered as his eyes swept over me quickly before looking away. I had been dressing down for so long, 'neglecting my looks' as my mum had called it, that I had completely forgotten about the effect that I had on men.

As we were all herded out into the rain afterwards, I noticed Deedee ahead of me, with another girl, shrieking as rain drops drenched her. Almost none of us had thought to bring umbrellas. I remembered, suddenly, that she was studying history and would be based in the same building. I caught up with her feeling inexplicably shy. It looked like she had made another friend already. The other girl had a yellow hood which was attached to a rain jacket, the sort of practical garment that parents are always trying to make you wear.

"Hi." I announced myself and the girl in the hood turned to me, a lick of garish yellow hair plastered over her wet face and my mouth went dry. I tried to kid myself frantically. Carrie. Carrie had yellow hair too but, firstly, Carrie was studying medicine and so would be on the other side of the campus and most significantly, Carrie was tiny and this girl had a heft to her, a familiar heft. Last seen over Enrique's shoulder in the murk of a Mexican nightclub, those dark jealous eyes, deceptively bovine.

"This is Zoe, she's doing History too." announced Deedee merrily, entirely oblivious of my inner turmoil. I don't know why we pretended not to know each other. At the time I thought that we were both in shock. Later, I had cause to reconsider.

"Hi Zoe!" I didn't recognise my voice. It sounded high and reedy. Why was she here? What was she doing here?

"Where are you staying?" I trilled

"One block away from you." Zoe stared at me from beneath her hood with a sardonic smile which Deedee couldn't see. "Block B."

Of course, Deedee would already have told her. I felt a sinking. Deedee chattered on, seemingly oblivious to the frosty atmosphere surrounding her companions. In any case, we were all helplessly negotiating the vicious onslaught of rain, the sort of rain which none of us were accustomed to. Wetly, we finally branched off at our respective accommodation blocks. It was Sunday and lessons would commence the following day. Deedee chatted all the way into our flat, no vestiges of hangover apparent on her. I, however, felt a vague nausea, a foreboding. I was cold and damp and prickly with discomfort. I had a terrible urge to go back to bed. Not this unmade, narrow, institutional bed but the warm messy one in Ben's flat that smelt of his weed and his sweat.

Chapter 21

Carrie had already been given a ton of reading to do. She rushed into the kitchen where Deedee and I were trying to warm up with a cup of tea, looking both hyped up and overwhelmed. Her shrewd dark eyes were glinting.

"Does anyone want to come to the library with me? I've got to get started on this lot, like straight away." I gazed bleakly at the sodden landscape beyond the bins. I didn't really want to go out into that again but I felt jittery and edgy and needed to keep moving. At the same time, I felt enormous pity for Carrie, so tiny and so far from home. Close up, she looked nothing like Zoe. Her hair was longer and a different shade, obviously dyed.

I dressed more sensibly this time and carried an umbrella. Carrie wore a green poncho which made her look like a minute elf. Like a kid dressing up on Halloween. We set off at a light jog, breathless and giggling, our trainers slipping on the sodden paths, our toes freezing. I tried really hard to stop thinking about Zoe. Surely, I reasoned, this place was big enough that I could avoid her? One of my feet felt wet, unbeknownst to me a hole must have formed in my shoe. We were a bit hysterical, probably still drunk. I swear that I could smell alcohol in my own sweat. I noticed a path branching off through a denser patch of wood on the right.

"Where do you think that goes?" I grabbed Carrie's arm, pointing.

She stopped and peered. There was nothing to see, the path vanished into blackness.

"Oh, that must be the way to the student union! Apparently, they have a cool bar, we should go there tonight."

"I hope the path is lit at night!" I laughed nervously.

"Oh, I'm sure it is, don't worry." Carrie patted me on the shoulder. She had to reach up to do it. I felt strongly that it should be vice versa, that I should be the one protecting her.

We arrived at the back entrance of the main building red of face and out of breath. Carrie looked pretty suddenly; her eyes luminous in her flushed face. The library was a massive room, more like a hall with a mezzanine situated to our left accessed by a spiral staircase. Students were milling around everywhere. There was a great concentration of them around the librarian's desk, chattering in loud whispers, trying to sort out their new cards. It all looked a bit too crowded for my liking. Suddenly, I couldn't be bothered to deal with it. The adrenalin seeped out of me and I followed Carrie like a dog, listlessly, to the Human Biology section. Once there, I thumbed through an anatomy book feeling stupid whilst Carrie dashed around, trying to get hold of the texts before her fellow med students found them. She had it on good authority that there was a limited supply.

I propped myself up against a table. Suddenly, a voice shocked me, close to my ear.

"You know that you're in the wrong section, don't you?"

James was standing very close, his voice deeper and more plummy even than before. I felt shy. I had no idea what to say. He looked older than he had from a distance. I could see the creases under his eyes but the skin on his cheeks looked touchable, smooth.

"I'm only joking!" He chuckled. "Don't look so worried!"

I made myself smile back. I don't know why I couldn't seem to form words. Something about his proximity had struck me dumb.

"Here, let me show you." His tone was jokey still, maybe a bit patronising and he touched me lightly on the shoulder. Where his fingers landed, I felt the material stick to me warmly. A pleasant heat.

He steered me towards the literature section and I looked around to inform Carrie, but she was nowhere to be seen.

"So," he looked at me appraisingly, "You look a bit older than the others?"

I glanced at him sharply but he chuckled.

"No offence intended! I just meant that you look more mature somehow."

I smiled to show that I wasn't offended but inside there was some turbulence.

"Yeah, I'm 19, I took a gap year."

"Right" he said lightly, "Did you have fun?"

"Kind of." I looked away and tried to laugh.

"Oh right, story for another day then!" He peered at me over his glasses, his eyes smiling.

"Here we are." he announced.

We were standing in the middle of the modern literature section. The books were piled high on the lofty shelves. Some librarians were balancing on ladders. I had only seen that in films and I stared at them.

"OK. See you in class." he turned rapidly, suddenly, and left. I felt lost, weirdly abandoned, I was even a little dizzy, something to do with the height of the shelves soaring above me. I thought that I had better pretend to be doing something constructive. I fumbled for my creased reading list which I had squashed into the pocket of my jeans and started locating books. It was harder than I thought and required a lot on concentration but it calmed me right down.

That evening we went to the student union bar. We didn't dress up. It was too cold and wet to even think about that. I hadn't realised quite what a remote, rural vibe this place would have. We had a quick shot of vodka and to line our stomachs, we very sensibly, made some pasta. We had all brought supplies of non-perishable foods from home and organised them all neatly in the cupboards and shelves with our names on them. There was a student supermarket located on campus, it was indicated on our maps, but none of us had been there yet.

I had temporarily forgotten about Zoe. Actually, I think that I was just blocking her out. She was something that I couldn't stand to remember. We were all exuberant in any case, excited, like proper young people. I felt comfortable around my flatmates. Happiness hovered oner me like a cloud.

I applied the teeniest bit of make-up; a sliver of lipstick, one coat of mascara, whereas, Carrie transformed herself completely. She disappeared into her room for about half an hour and then reappeared looking almost unrecognisable and much older. She'd applied a heavy layer of foundation and pink blusher sat garishly on her cheeks. Her eyes were ringed with dark grey shadow. It didn't look great. She looked like a kid playing dress up with her mum's make-up. We all told her that she looked lovely, of course. Deedee wore a substantial amount of make-up too, but then I had already got the impression that she always did, night or day. Julian sat at the kitchen table watching us and waiting, the bottle of vodka before him. I don't believe that he made any effort at all, he didn't even change his jeans or shirt.

At last, we were ready to go.

Chapter 22

We set off down the dark path which we had seen earlier. Other students were pouring out of their accommodation blocks and going the same way so it felt busy and sociable, not creepy at all. There were lights too. Old-fashioned lanterns hung at decent intervals but beyond them was dense foliage and pure black. It took about twenty minutes of fast giggly walking and then we arrived at a very ornate, archaic looking structure which looked like a pub from the Victorian era. It had heavy beams made of aged timber and pretty, mullioned windows. It somehow managed to be both imposingly large and inside, surprisingly snug. The bar was situated next to a more workaday building, also cavernous but more similar to our concrete accommodation blocks. It was there, I surmised that other, everyday student union stuff went on. Loudly, in the background, we could hear the babbling of a brook or river. It was strangely deafening, the noise seemed to vibrate around my head. Inside we sat in a warm nook drinking cheap beer. It all felt very cosy. There was even a log fire and everyone's faces took on a rosy pink glow. The music was raucous inside and the volume drowned out the din of the river or whatever it was.

"What do you think it is?" I asked Carrie.

"Let's go and see. I bet we could see something through the window."

We weaved our way through the drunk red-faced students swaying gently in groups which constantly dispersed and reformed, like waves slipping back and forth. At the back of the structure was a solid glass door which was locked with a heavy chain. Beyond it, we could see an extensive wooden deck and the cacophony of water was audible once more.

"It's a river." announced a deep voice next to me. I jumped, shocked, I thought Carrie was right behind me. I turned to see a very lanky boy looming over me. I only came up to his shoulder and I had to bend my neck right back to see his face.

"I saw it this morning!" he continued excitedly. His face had the ubiquitous rosy glow and his blue eyes gleamed enthusiastically.

"It was all bubbly and rough, you know, like one of those rivers that you go white water rafting down!"

I had never been white water rafting but I could sort of picture what he meant. I turned back to where Carrie had been but she must have gone back to our table.

"You live with Julian, don't you?" asked the boy unexpectedly "He's with me in the music department. We actually went to school together. Did he tell you?"

"Um, no." Julian had insinuated that his school days were unhappy ones but had not mentioned any particular individuals by name.

"Was he your friend?" I asked the boy

He looked shifty, suddenly, his eyes focussed on something over my head.

"Kind of." he muttered. I sensed that the conversation was over, I wanted it to be over, and I turned to leave.

"Hang on!" He reached out and grabbed my arm. I looked at his fingers which were long and slim, a musician's fingers.

"What's your name?" I really wanted to get away from him then, I didn't like him.

"Lisa." I mumbled. Shaking his arm off, I made my way back to my new friends.

"Making friends?" Deedee looked up at me and winked.

"That guy was so tall!" Carrie was already slurring her words. To Carrie, he must have looked like a giant. I was irritated that she'd abandoned me there with a stranger but I didn't say anything. Her eye make-up was smeared on her cheek, she looked like a panda.

"Was that Dylan?" asked Julian. His voice seemed casual but there was a tightness to it.

"I didn't catch his name, but I didn't like him much."

"No, you shouldn't." said Julian grimly. "Definitely not!"

I waited for him to offer an explanation but he looked down and went silent. We had a few more drinks and then made our way back 'home', our arms hooked around each other's waists. I was totally relieved not to have seen Zoe, hopefully she would keep out of my way. I felt a mellow warmth, an optimism. When I saw a dark shape skitter past in the wood next to the path, I almost thought that I had imagined it.

"Did you see that?" I asked Julian, who was next to me. He looked concerned.

"No, but I'll keep my eyes peeled, it's probably just a squirrel."

Somehow, that didn't reassure me. It was too big to be a squirrel, I knew.

Chapter 23

The first person whom I saw the next day, was Carrie. She was standing in the doorway of my room staring at me. She hadn't cleaned all her make-up off well and there were black smudges still, under her eyes. I struggled to wake up. I felt as if I was trying to defy gravity.

"Is everything alright?" I asked her, rubbing my eyes.

"Um yeah, I just wanted to let you know that I'm leaving now."

She still stood there, transferring her meagre weight from foot to foot like a child. The sky outside the window was dark grey.

"Ok." I smiled "Have a good day!"

She left, finally, and yawning I headed for the kitchen. Julian was sprawled in one of the chairs, one hand clutching a mug. He looked pale and dishevelled.

"Couldn't really sleep…" he mumbled, glancing up at me.

"Oh?"

"I kept thinking about Dylan, I can't believe that bastard is here!"

"Yeah, I know what you mean, not about Dylan I mean, but there's someone who has shown up here that I'd rather forget too."

Deedee walked in then and the subject was changed. She hadn't drawn her eyebrows in yet and her mad pink hair was sticking up all over the place.

"Hey Abs, did you see the message for you?"

There was one payphone shared between three flats on each floor. It was situated inconveniently in the corridor and was only ever answered if someone happened to be passing and could be bothered.

She rubbed her eyes, which looked oddly naked.

"Um yeah, there was a note on the kitchen table, somebody called."

"Who?"

She screwed up her nose, thinking. I started to feel irritated.

"Um sorry, I forgot."

I tried to look neutral, as if I didn't care. I scanned the table for a neglected note amongst the debris; dirty mugs, ashtrays, notebooks and pens. No, nothing.

I was just drying my hair after my shower when she burst into my room.

"I remember!" she yelled triumphantly, "It was Ben!"

"Oh, thanks."

I felt guilty. I hadn't given Ben much thought since I arrived, there was too much going on. I got dressed and went to phone him. I knew that even if he was working, the dayshifts didn't start until later.

"Where were you?" he blurted out as soon as he'd picked up the phone.

"What?" I was astonished at his tone. I had never heard him sound so agitated.

"I called! You weren't there! Where were you? I just want to know!"

I started to explain the tricky phone in corridor situation but he didn't want to listen. He interrupted me and there was an edge to his voice, a hostility, but also a desperation.

"I just wanted to talk to you, like really, really wanted to talk to you!"

"Why?" I asked, baffled. I felt merely exhausted and indifferent, totally detached from this neediness and urgency.

"You're my girlfriend aren't you, aren't you?" I'd had enough then. He was loud and fierce, he had morphed into a stranger who I didn't want to know.

"You know what," I told him "I'll talk to you when you've calmed down."

With a gentle click, I put the receiver down and then stood there staring at it. There had to be some explanation. Maybe he'd smoked something dodgy. I could practically hear, in his voice, the toxins oozing through his pores. I fully expected the phone to ring again whilst I was standing there staring at it. It was an old-fashioned device which had its own little metal shelf, purpose built I thought. It had a chipped scarlet plastic coating and a dialler that looked murky with the residue from hundreds of grubby fingers. It must have borne witness, through the years, to all kinds of angst and drama.

It didn't ring and I went off to my lectures. They were not with James on that day but with other lecturers. I was engaged and distracted and totally forgot about both Ben and Zoe until I returned to the flat mid-afternoon. Spookily, just as I was on the way to our front door, the phone was ringing. My heart jolted. I ignored it. It might have been Ben but in that instant, I didn't want to know.

The next few days were peaceful. After the initial overexcitement and holiday type excess of the first days, we calmed right down. We went to our lectures, we wandered over to the library to borrow books. We went on a joint excursion to the student supermarket, which was fun and we were childishly gleeful and silly about it. We had decided to plan meals for the week together. The supermarket was gloriously cheap and scrappy. Very few items were laid out on shelves, mainly they were left out in open cardboard boxes in plastic packaging which we had to rip through ourselves. The novelty of this entertained us hugely. We overstocked on the cheap greens, of course. Within a few days our kitchen would be ripe with the odour of rotting vegetation. We did manage a few meals together but our schedules didn't really overlap. Mine and Deedee's were similar but Carrie was either in the classroom or in the local hospital full-time and Julian had some strangely placed early evening classes which interfered with dinner time.

That week, I tried to forget about Ben. I told myself that I would call him when he calmed down but days passed and I found that I didn't want to think about him. The phone remained mercifully quiet and when it did ring it was never for me. My most regular companions during that time were Deedee and Julian and we developed a jokey camaraderie. Carrie, it seemed, was always studying. I met other students of course. I'd chat to them in whispers during class and in a normal voice during the breaks. I even got used to the foul weather. We were always so wrapped up that we looked like Eskimos, just our eyes showing. I think we all kind of felt like we were in another country, exotic and alien. The savagery of the landscape didn't feel like England at all.

On Thursday, I had a lecture with James. It was about Frankenstein and other gothic literature. It took place in the actual lecture hall, although the vast majority of lectures seemed to happen in normal classrooms, just like school. James looked noble standing at the cistern as if he was a fine-featured actor playing a role. It was crowded and he barely glanced at me, but the following day, and on a fortnightly basis, I had tutor group with him. Just me and two other boys.

Tutor group took place in his surprisingly spacious office. I had imagined something cosy, something I had seen in a film, with a roaring fire and leather armchairs. His office was nothing like that. It was vast and modern and bland and functional and we sat on padded office chairs in front of his desk as if we were about to be interviewed. He didn't pay any particular attention to me. He was friendly and warm and we discussed modern day parallels to Gothic horror. I got a bit too drawn in to my imagination at that point. A showreel of images ran through my mind; Zoe's ghoulish face, Penny's terrible dehydrated lips in the desert and the gun, waving at us shockingly. That split second when you think it's a prop and then realise that it's not. A toy, but not a toy. I had all this in my brain, tumbling about. I started sweating and then all three were looking at me. The two boys curious and James concerned. I had remembered, suddenly, with a vivid thump in my chest, that Zoe was still around, and not only around, but possibly near me.

"Are you OK, Abby?"

"Oh fine, fine!" I gulped, wiping my hand across my damp forehead.

"It's just kind of hot in here."

"No, it's not!" snorted one of the boys and I could see James give him a nasty look, his eyes hard.

"Yes. Yes, it is a bit stuffy, why don't you step out for a minute and get some air?"

I felt shaky as I stood up and the soulless corridor was abandoned. It was just me and the flickering strip lights overhead. Everyone was in class. I felt the neon burn my eyes, it pained me. Outside was a shock of wind. I felt my sweat dry coldly beneath my hairline. I lifted up my face. It was a relief to feel empty then, a relief.

By the time that I returned to the room, the boys had gone and James was there alone. He was leaning over his desk looking at some papers. He looked as if he was just about to leave and then realised that he had better wait for me. When I entered the room, he moved towards me and put a hand on my shoulder.

"Are you alright? Do you want to talk about it?"

I gulped. The weight of his fingers on my shoulder felt tender and warmth spread through me. The ugly light overhead emitted a vague hissing sound. He moved backwards then, as if respectfully, maybe he didn't want to be seen crossing a line. I felt an intense compulsion to lean into his chest. There was something about that preppy striped shirt, the expensive looking jacket that drew me in. Even in the neon glare, his skin looked rosy. But I didn't move and neither did he and we separated in the ordinary way.

Back at 'home', I called Ben. I felt intense pity for him and guilt, of course I felt guilt. I wanted someone else. Finally, I was honest with myself, it was obvious. Ben sounded happy to hear from me and normal, above all, reassuringly normal.

"What on earth was wrong with you last time?" I asked tentatively. "You sounded kind of weird?"

"Yeah, sorry, there was this bad patch of pills going around. I took two. Well, I took one than I forgot and took another."

"O.K." I sighed. I really wanted to point out the obvious, namely, that he shouldn't be taking pills at all. I felt so far away from all that here. I knew that I had been involved in it all myself, but now it seemed ridiculous and childish and above all, pointless. I hadn't seen any drugs here. Most people seemed geeky and wholesome. I couldn't picture them here somehow; not only the drugs themselves but the ferrety, cynical, poor people that went with them. I had somehow, in a short space of time, reinvented myself as a snobby, middle-class student.

Chapter 24

There definitely was a geeky vibe. The work was pretty hard. It had been a good long time, by then, since I had written an essay and my first attempt was mediocre to say the least. 'Bad' would be a more honest assessment, below par and substandard. Unfortunately, the essay had been for Sylvia who, I realised then, was stricter than I had imagined a professor would be at university. I don't know what I had expected, I was very naïve. I think I had pictured that it would be more convivial, intellectual chats over cups of tea. Anyway, she kept me behind after one of her lectures and told me that my work needed to improve. She said it very firmly. I got quite worried and started working much harder.

Deedee told me that she had arrived at a similar conclusion.

"Maybe, I should have applied to a more fun university?" she rolled her eyes at me. I don't think that she was joking, not entirely.

As a consequence of all the surprising but necessary hard work, we only went to the student bar at weekends, as one night out tended to wipe us out the following day. The following Saturday was an organised outing to celebrate my birthday, but it was also some kind of anniversary of an important date in the history of the university. There was going to be a special night to celebrate. Everyone had planned to go anyway, special night or not, they didn't really need an excuse. To be honest, I don't remember what the special anniversary was, but when we got to the bar and started peeling off our Eskimo layers, we noticed the university insignia on little flags everywhere. I would later discover that those same little flags were also waved about at rugby and football matches. The insignia was a tiger roaring against a black background. It was kind of ugly and the whole flag thing, patriotism and the herd tribal thing had never meant anything to me.

Anyway, there were all these ridiculous little flags everywhere and the ubiquitous already-drunk people. A group of muscular boys (Rugby?) and another of muscular girls (Rugby?) who were affiliated to each other in some way, were drinking pints near the bar. Beer seemed to be the unofficial choice of tipple for every sports team regardless of sex.

Our little group of misfits found a table in our usual area, in the far corner near the locked door leading to the terrace. Even above the raucous din of music and drunk shouting, you could hear the angry burbling of the river. We drank tequila shots and then vodka with various mixers. We got drunk pretty quickly. Every time someone lifted a glass, everyone yelled "Happy Birthday Abs!"

Carrie was wearing her excessive doll-like make-up and started collapsing onto me as if she couldn't hold herself up. She started to annoy me, so I went for a little stroll to the bar to get some water. People moved aside for me as they always had, with the heavily drunk boy groups ogling and mumbling under their breath. Deep in my head, I heard the chant "Mamacita Mamacita!" and when one of them grabbed my arm, I snatched myself out of his reach with violence. If I had been a cat, I would have been spitting and hissing.

"Woah! Easy tiger!" one of them guffawed and there was snorting laughter all around and I put my head down to push through and return to the relative safety of my flatmates and when I looked up Zoe was right there in front of me. Immediately, the phrase 'one of them' sprang to mind. She was wearing no make-up. She looked pale, plain and hostile. She was wearing a rugby top.

"Do you play rugby?" I asked, my voice a bit shaky. It was the first thing that I thought of. I was shocked to have come across her so suddenly, as if the rugby boys had conjured her up from thin air with the express purpose of detaining me.

"No, netball. But we hang out with the rugby team" she said smugly with a self-important little smirk, as if she expected me to be jealous.

"Right" I looked around urgently, wanting to be gone from there, but I was surrounded by burly, sweaty people. She stood in front of me holding her pint, a slick of yellow hair plastered to her forehead. I felt drunk. Bile rose in my throat. She stared at me. She had the same creepy stare as her brother.

"Do you ever hear from Emma?"

I turned away then and just started to barge through them, my forearms up like a shield. It was so loud and they all seemed to loom over me, leering and catcalling.

"Where are you going, beautiful?"

"Come here, why the rush!"

"Give us a kiss!"

I regretted the sliver of lipstick I was wearing. Why would I make myself more attractive for this? My heart pounded in my eardrums,

"MAMACITA" I heard, "MAMACITA!" Heat engulfed me, my throat closed up and then I was standing in front of my flatmates sobbing and Julian sprang up and first and put his arm around me.

"OK. Ok, what happened? Shall I take you back home?"

I nodded, my face wet with tears and snot. We left the others there. Fortunately, our exit was not blocked. I calmed down in the cold and the silence outside. The weather was heavy with ice, it seeped in everywhere. We needed all our energy to focus on keeping warm, our muscles were tense and rigid. The woods to the side of us had their own muttering music; the whistling wind through the foliage, the scurrying of tiny creatures, the snapping of twigs. I didn't turn to see if there was anything there that night, I had enough demons in my head.

Chapter 25

I kept talking to Ben about once a week and we got on well enough after that initial weird outburst. I hoped that he would avoid the pills and learn his lesson. It would have been too much to expect him to forego the narcotics entirely. Honestly, I no longer felt much for him. He was a close friend whom I had left behind. I didn't vocalize that but I kind of assumed that we were having a natural, unspoken tapering out. I never invited him up to stay and he, in turn, never asked to visit. I looked back on time spent drugged in that slovenly flat with a shudder. It's not as if the conditions in my current accommodation were much more sanitary, it's more that the people were more intelligent and I was changing, had changed already.

That is how I rationalized it all, so that when the affair with James started, it didn't feel as if I was betraying Ben. Maybe I was kidding myself, but that is how I felt. It felt logical. I was not surprised that James was attracted to me. What astonished me was that I actually wanted something to happen. As it was, nothing did happen until November. There was a lot of studious graft and a lot of innocent flirting. Carrie increasingly got on my nerves. She was often hard at work but when she was at home, she stuck to me like glue, following me around with her soulful little face like a puppy.

At the bar, where we'd still go at weekends, I now knew better than to leave my friends, my tribe. We'd always sit detached from the rabble and I'd see Zoe from a distance with the sporty gang, I'd glance quickly and turn away, my heart already rising in my throat. My friends would often tell me that she was staring at me though. Another person who was getting on my nerves was Dylan. He would lumber over to our table in the bar, his long gangly form visible from far off. I would give him short shrift and Julian would glare at him with such ferocity that he would back away. However, Julian was rarely with me during the day, and sometimes Dylan would loom ahead of me on a murky path, like a massive spider, blocking the way. He would ask me lots of questions about myself as if I was being interrogated. I would be trying to dodge past him and answering in monosyllables but he would never let me leave, his limbs seemed to extend everywhere like tentacles. He'd keep repeating;

"We really have to get together soon, when are you free?" Time after time I'd have to solidify my anger into strength and push past him and jog away, all the while searching desperately for some acquaintance to latch onto. He would never bother me when I was with someone that he didn't know.

The way that James and I got together in the end, felt like a cliché. Even as it was happening, it felt as if it was being engineered. It had, about it, an artificial edge. Sometimes, I imagined that we were bad actors in a Mexican soap opera, with all the tired lines and the bad melodrama.

On a dark wintry afternoon, (one of many, of course, they were all dark and wintry), I had left my red woollen scarf in his office after a tutorial. I don't think that I left it deliberately, not consciously anyway. He looked like a figure in a painting running after me in the gloom, the scarf, a red ribbon, trailing behind him as he ran. He had it wrapped around his wrist. There was no one about anywhere, only the trees and the distant gurgling of the omnipresent river, still unseen. He wrapped the scarf gently around my shoulders and pulled me towards him. It was a skilful move, romantic, but it felt scripted even then.

We kissed and arranged to meet later at his dwelling. He lived in the caretaker's cottage near the student supermarket. Bizarrely, the caretaker himself lived in the attic of the main building. The other teachers had digs in the nearby town. It was because he didn't have a car, he explained, that he had been set up in the cottage. It all sounded a bit shady to me, a bit odd, but right then it was certainly convenient. Once we had kissed, feelings escalated quickly, the innocence evaporated into the air. He was quite forceful, I thought, right from the start. I was a decision he'd made and he was entitled to see it through.

The caretaker's cottage smelt musty and was filled with grubby, broken things. There was dilapidated furniture and what looked like old-fashioned sports equipment: nets, rackets, lacrosse sticks. Half of the living room was piled high with such stuff.

"Don't you mind?" I asked him, gingerly picking my way through. He just shrugged.

"You should have seen where I was before!"

I raised my eyebrows and asked him where he had been before, but he ignored me and turned away. Outside the surety of the classroom, there was a caginess about him. His stories, rarely recounted, were full of missing parts.

After the clutter of the living room, his bedroom felt shockingly austere, like that of a monk. There was nothing in it except a double bed and a wardrobe. Not even a bedside table or lamp, just the harsh overhead light. I squinted as we went in. There was nothing soft or romantic about this house, it felt cold. He must have sensed my growing unease because he brought in a candle in a bottle and a stereo and put on a popular alternative CD. He wanted to prove that we were on the same page, I guess, despite the age difference. He was setting the scene and he was accomplished at it. I asked him if there had been other students before me. I couldn't see his face at that moment. The candle was in the middle of the floor. We were lying on our backs in bed, our sides touching. He didn't say anything straight away and then he told me that he had only been at Pembridge for two terms, that he had arrived in the Spring. Which wasn't what I had asked.

"Where were you before that then?"

"Another university on the South coast."

He clammed up again and then we started to touch one another. His skin was very soft for a man and he was clearly far more experienced than Ben, a completely different animal.

That's how it began.

I never stayed the entire night there but he would walk me part of the way back at 1 or 2am. He would leave me in the cold and the dark, afraid that we would be seen together. He pretended it was mutually beneficial but fear would often accompany me through the night like a loyal dog. He always said "You'll be safe here, it's very safe here." I think he was trying to reassure himself. I would run after he left me. The paths would often still have groups of students on them, usually lurching about drunkenly. The vintage street lanterns gave the place a nostalgic air, something like Victorian London in the fog. I would run fast and usually when I arrived home, sweaty and panting, Deedee and Julian would still be up and drinking in the kitchen and the atmosphere would be convivial and warm. I would have a drink or a cup of tea and I would feel as if I had arrived home after an illicit adventure, which, I suppose, is what it was.

My flatmates were the only people who knew about James and they had been sworn to secrecy. In lectures and in tutorials, he acted more distant to me than to the others, like a double bluff. So distant, in fact, that I struggled to believe that he had any feelings for me at all. Sometimes I imagined that our relationship existed only in my head.

It was around that time that I finally decided to confront Carrie. I felt that it would be a difficult conversation, painful but necessary for my own sanity, like ripping a plaster off. I asked her if she wanted a cup of tea. She had been studying in her room with the door open. I always felt as if she was waiting for me, any excuse and she would leap up to be with me, like a loyal dog.

"Carrie," I began when we were both sitting at the kitchen table, I lit a cigarette and exhaled, "I wanted to talk to you, because well…I am having some personal issues…you may have noticed, I mean, it is kind of obvious! I do seem to be dragging all of you into them! I am sorry about that…"

She stared at me bemused and I realised that I was rambling on and tried to focus.

She leant forward and took a cigarette out of my packet and I stared transfixed. I hadn't seen her smoke before. It seemed incongruous, wrong somehow, like watching a child smoke.

She saw me staring and grinned with her bad teeth,

"Just occasionally, I give in to the urge. I shouldn't, of course, it's definitely frowned upon in medical circles! I've always loved smoking, though, love it. I am a smoker deep down. In my heart."

It was that kind of comment that cemented things for me, confirmed for me that something was off about her.

"Anyway," I ploughed on, "My point is…what I'm trying to say is…I really need some more space to, you know, work through all the issues, and…"

To my horror, her eyes filled with tears. She held the cigarette ineptly in her tiny fist. More than ever, she looked exactly like a small girl pretending to be a grown up.

"Oh no!" I blustered, "Please don't cry! There's nothing to cry about! We can still be friends, I think you have misunderstood, it's not that I don't want to hang out with you, it's just that…"

I gave up and took a deep drag. I felt like I was just making things worse and suddenly, I didn't have the energy to extricate myself from the messiness of this conversation.

"It's just…" She wiped her tiny nose on the sleeve of her oversized jumper, took a drag of her cigarette. We both watched the smoke emerge in little clouds as she exhaled. "It's just…you remind me very much of a friend of mine, back in the States."

She tried to get herself together, sat up straighter even, stubbed out her cigarette, pulled her sleeves over her tiny hands.

"She looked just like you, just maybe not as tall, but the same beautiful face, the same hair. She could be your sister!"

"Oh, OK, where is she, your friend? Is she still there? Is she studying medicine too?"

"She's dead." Carrie stated flatly and she reached instinctively for another cigarette. I recognised the set of her face, the deep pain in it and I felt a cold chill run through me.

"What happened? Um…only if you want to talk about it, of course?" I didn't really want to know. At that precise moment, I wanted to be away from her, alone in my room.

"Well, the short story is that she killed herself. Her name was, is Casey. She was pre-med, she knew what she was doing so she took an overdose of the right pills which she knew were going to be successful. Successful is the wrong word, of course, but you know what I mean."

She gave me a hard look then which I couldn't decipher.

"And she was, successful. She died."

"I'm so sorry to hear that!" I really was. My American twin somewhere, lost. It could easily have been me.

"Would you like to know why?" she was still staring at me with her unfathomable uncomfortable gaze.

Not really, I thought, No, not at all. I would very much like to go back to my room.

"Yes, sure, why?"

"She was raped at a party, by multiple boys. It happened in our last year at high school. She was drunk but obviously she didn't know what they were going to do, she trusted them. Two of them were her particularly close friends. They had lived on her street her whole life. They had walked to school with her, together, since they were tiny. They had walked her to the party too. It was nearby.

"Didn't she report them?"

"Of course, she did! She went into the police station that very night. They didn't believe her. They sent her home. They said they didn't believe her because she had been drinking and ergo, she couldn't possibly be clear as to exactly what had happened."

"How drunk was she? Not that it justifies anything of course!"

"Not very, that's the thing. She was the type of girl who would only ever have a couple of beers at a party. There was this one boy that she fancied there and it was him that she went upstairs with…it wasn't one of the boys she walked to school with, but it was a friend of theirs and she thought that she could trust him."

Dee appeared in the doorway at that point, took one look at us and backed out again wordlessly. I gave her a quick look over Carrie's head. I don't know what she took it to mean, but she nodded.

"OK…" she sighed almost in exasperation, as if I had been questioning her instead of just sitting there dumbly smoking.

"This is what happened. I was supposed to go that night but I was sick, my tonsils were swollen. It was something that afflicted me often…anyway I couldn't go, so, as I said, she went with these two boys who lived on her street. I mean, it was…I don't have a word for it…to her, they were like her brothers and the party was actually at a girl's house. She was a girl in our year, we didn't know her very well but she was known for hosting frequent parties as her parents were often out of town and known to have a lackadaisical approach to discipline and rules. Basically, they knew what she got up to, locked away their valuables and didn't really care about the mess. She was one of the cool girls and Casey and I rarely got invited but that time we were, unfortunately, and under normal circumstances, she would never have gone without me. Even with her two, what she tragically called, her bodyguards. Even with those two bastards. We always went everywhere together. We weren't in the cool set and we were kind of intimidated by them. However, on that particular evening, she found out that this boy she'd been obsessed with for ages, Rob, was going to be there, so, despite me not going, she decided to go.

It was the weirdest feeling I had that evening. I was sitting in the den with my parents watching some crap; my mum had just given me something for my throat and was making me a hot drink… I got this creepy cold sensation that came over me. It was physical. I presumed that I was even sicker than I thought, but I had never had it before and I never had it again after that. Most people don't believe me when I tell them about it, but it was as if I knew…something…my body knew, that something was badly wrong. That something dreadful was about to happen. We were really close, see? Too close, people thought. They were always making jokes that we were lesbians and my mum was always hinting, not-so-subtly, that maybe I should branch out and find some more friends, that I shouldn't put all my eggs in one basket…etcetera…I guess she couldn't have foreseen, nobody could have guessed the consequences of…"

She gulped and I prepared us both a cup of tea. In hers, I put two spoons of sugar. She enclosed both tiny hands around the mug. For a second, the steam obscured her pale face. I wondered if she had always looked this sickly or if her wan appearance was a result of this disaster which had befallen her.

"So, Casey went to the party with her two best buddies, whom she considered to be her best buddies after me. I can't say their names because when I do, a rage comes into me and I feel like…I feel like I will combust or something…because I knew them too, of course. I had known them my whole life, and I hadn't seen anything evil in them or even anything remotely predatory. They had always seemed harmless to me, guileless, a bit geeky even! How ironic is that?"

"They all drank, of course." Carrie continued, lighting another cigarette, "Casey was so excited to see Rob. She was sure that something would happen…there had been eye contact and flirting for ages in school. He was pre-med too. That just added to her infatuation. She thought that he was perfect for her. I wondered at the time, if she was so excited that she drank more than was usual for her, but she swore to me, the next day, that she didn't…she had two beers. That's exactly what she said to me. She said; Carrie I just had two beers! Two bottles of Mexican beer! You know me! You know that I'm a lightweight."

I thought of myself, sitting on the bed in my room in Elena's flat. I could taste the Mexican beer on my lips as Carrie spoke, the memory of it.

"They must have drugged her! That's the only explanation…that's the…OK. Let me recap a bit." She took a deep breath.

"Casey told me that as soon as she got there, Rob started flirting with her. He was glued to her side, that's exactly how she described it and she felt that hazy blissful dreamlike feeling…like something that you've been wanting for a while is actually happening and you can't quite believe it and you know that you'll want to savour the memory after… It was perfect for a while and then she felt…weird…a bit dizzy…not drunk, worse than drunk was how she described it. Coincidentally…ha! Rob told her that she didn't look well, that she should lie down. He took her to a room upstairs, a bedroom, she has no recollection of it… there were some coats on the bed and she kind of collapsed on them. They were a bit damp as it had been raining earlier. She felt the dampness seep on to her skin. It was a big house, there were lots of rooms. Rob had shut the door of the room but almost immediately it opened and some other people came in. She had her eyes closed because she felt so sick and dizzy, but she could hear their voices and she recognised them and she wasn't remotely worried. They were laughing and whispering then, she remembered thinking that that was a bit odd, because, well, why? But still, she wasn't worried. She never would have imagined that she would have cause to be. Then, and then…she thinks that she passed out for a bit and the next thing she felt hands on her everywhere, and she knew that it was more than one pair of hands because they were everywhere at once and she felt, not paralysed exactly, but very weak and floppy as if it was really hard to move, really difficult to get her limbs to respond…Basically, she was stuck to the bed whilst hands, she thinks three pairs, roamed all over her, roughly, grabbing, and then they started to pull down the jeans she was wearing. She could feel them pulling at the jeans around her ankles, then the whoosh of air on her skin as her body, her flesh, was exposed. The dampness from the wet coats, the cold. All this time, she was trying to scream but the sound just wasn't there. It was as if someone had lowered the volume on her voice so that it couldn't be heard…it was just this pathetic whimper. She was on her back, still on top of the coats, the buttons and zippers digging into her back, and they were laughing and grunting above her and she could feel this terrible ripping pain because that was the first time for her. She could hear them egging each other on and one of them panted, on top of her and in her ear, "You're so beautiful, so beautiful!" and she wanted to spit on him but she couldn't even do that. It was one of the boys on her road. She recognised the aftershave that he was wearing…she had teased him about it on the way to the party. She had specifically joked around with him and with the other boy saying that the girls wouldn't be able to resist the aftershave…it was one of the fancy expensive ones. Right then, of course, it served to sicken her further. She willed her body to vomit on them but her body wouldn't comply. She lay there dumbly and stupidly, like some 'fucking cow being slaughtered' is how she put it to me afterwards, just exactly like that.

Eventually they left her. One of them put her knickers back on, as if he was doing her a big fucking favour, but not her jeans, and she thinks that she passed out again. The next time she came too, she felt wet and sticky and then vomit did come and she managed to put her head to one side before it gushed out of her everywhere and a girl came, actually the girl whose house it was. Initially she was screaming at Casey because of the vomit and the mess, the stench must have been horrible, but when she put the light on, she must have seen that actually…well…seen…

To her credit, this girl, Marie, did help as much as anyone could have then. The boys had long gone and she got Casey up somehow and gave her water. By now it was really late, but Casey had told her parents that she was staying at mine…it was something we often did when we wanted to stay out late. Anyway, no one came looking and Marie got it together and kicked all the stragglers out and got her and Casey a cab to the police station.

It was the nail in the coffin, Casey told me afterwards, that was the very phrase that she used, the way that she was treated in that police station; the nail in the coffin."

Carrie looked at me again, that odd sharp look;

"I wondered if she was planning it, even then, when she used that phrase to me just a few days after it happened. It was a strange phrase to use. Not one that I had heard her use before."

"What happened in the police station?" I asked with an odd mixture of curiosity and dread.

"They completely dismissed her! The desk sergeant chuckled when she walked in with Marie, chuckled! He said, in a tired, patronising tone, "OK, what is it, love?" As if it was bound to be a waste of time or nonsense. She started to tell him and he interrupted her before she'd finished and he accused her, that's what it sounded like, an accusation, he said; "But you'd been drinking! Therefore, you can't remember accurately, therefore, it's invalid!" He said all that and Casey cried, sobbed, and Marie was horrified and they hadn't even got any further than the front desk!

"Just take her home love." that bastard said to Marie, and Casey, by then was just in bits, Marie told me, curled up, hysterical on the floor and Marie, well neither of them, could argue with the police. They didn't have the words, that was how they felt. They had no way of knowing how to go about challenging that kind of authority…It would have been hard for a male, for a female it felt impossible. Marie took Casey home and she slunk in without her parents noticing and they were surprised to see her there the next day as they had thought that she was staying at mine of course. She pretended to be sick for a few days, well she was really sick, in a worse way that anyone realised and her parents never found out, not until after she had, after she had… well after it was over and they can't get over it, I am told, they just can't. They are at least challenging the police. Marie told them all she knew, all that she saw on the night, gave them the names. At least that. I went to see her about four days after it had happened. I had been surprised not to hear from her, she had been so thrilled about seeing Rob…I had been excited for her! That was the irony! She told me the whole story…told me that she couldn't leave the house, couldn't bear the thought of seeing the two boys on her street, her so-called friends, couldn't actually bear the thought of anything, that's what she told me. I worried of course, but I didn't panic enough! I will never forgive myself for that! I should have alerted her parents right then! We should have been watching her twenty-four hours a day! In many ways it is my fault…that is how I feel."

"I think women are often made to feel as if things are their fault." I told her and I knew in that instant that it was true.

She looked up at me then, almost hopeful. Her eyes were red and watery. Right then, she looked a bit rodent-like and I instantly felt guilty for the thought.

"She killed herself, with the tablets, exactly a week after the rape. Her mum found her in her bed in the morning, completely cold."
"That must have been horrendous."

"Yes, it was. She will never get over it. I will never get over it. I couldn't even make it to the funeral. It was as if my legs wouldn't work. I was so weak, shaking and crying and my legs absolutely wouldn't work...I don't know what her parents thought about my absence. Probably, they were so devastated that they didn't notice. I left shortly after; I came here because I wanted to get as far from there as possible. I actually believed, I still believe, that if I see those two boys again I will kill them. I dream about it, I fantasize about it. It is all I want. Ergo, I don't think that I can ever go back."

"Not Rob? You don't want to kill him?"

"Oh, I hate that bastard too, naturally, but there's something about the other two in particular, the way that they pretended to be her friends. That seems, to me, to be the worst crime of all. It's...almost impossible for me to trust any men now."

There was a deep silence then for some time as we both stared outside the window at the outline of the industrial bins in the encroaching gloom.

Dee then knocked tentatively on the door. We knew it was her as she opened it immediately without waiting for a response and we could see a vibrant lock of hair. Carrie nodded at her slowly and I smiled and after a while normality, such as it was, ensued.

Chapter 26

In the meantime, back home, it seemed that my mum and dad were getting on very well and that there was the possibility of a reconciliation. That was what my dad said anyway. Clearly, she had not been completely honest with him yet, or told him the story which she had recounted to me. I spoke to them both on a weekly basis, separately, and I didn't quite get the same vibe from my mum. She was far more reserved, circumspect, in her observations concerning their relationship. I got the feeling that he was so desperate to get back with her that he was prepared to accept any crumb of hope that she offered. What seemed happily more probable though, was that Jack was on his way out. Mum told me categorically that he was getting on her nerves, but rather than return to my dad, I got the impression that she wanted to be alone.

I never spoke to my brother directly, but apparently, he had got himself a serious girlfriend, Caitlin.

"Too serious!" stated my mum, whatever that meant. Also, "He does whatever she says." Ironic really, considering that mum had always had dad wrapped around her little finger.

I missed them during those chats. I missed our cosy cluttered house with its low ceilings and familiar smells. At Penbridge, sometimes, the outdoors seemed too vast, too wild and unpredictable and sparsely populated. The unseen burbling river, the giant trees, dense and whispering and looming over us.

A month or so after James and I had got together, I was confronted on the path by Dylan. It was close to the Christmas break and there was a holiday atmosphere. All the communal buildings were decked out with fairy lights and trees and tinsel. I was in too relaxed a mood, that was why I didn't see him approach. He stood before me suddenly. His angular head blocked out the sun which was glaring that day, sparkling over a wintry frost.

"I know you're seeing your tutor." he stated in a mocking tone.

I stopped still and glared at him. Always, in the back of my head, like tickertape, ran the advice that you've got to stand up to bullies or they never back down. My fists were clenched at my side.

"You know nothing at all!" I hissed.

"He's not all that he seems, you know." He bent down towards me, his mouth a sarcastic sneer.

"You need to ask him where he was before and what he did there."

"Piss off!" I retorted in disgust and turning, jogged briskly away, but I felt the faint niggling of unease.

It was true that James was very reticent, even evasive about his past. Although we had become physically very intimate as a couple, the fact was that I knew no more about his past than I had done right at the start. That evening was our last night together before I went home. He wasn't going home which should have alerted me to something being amiss but I was too young and self-absorbed to find it weird. He said that he didn't get along with his family and I took it at face value. He seemed like an attractive man. He was gregarious and super bright but beneath the surface he was oddly isolated, a loner.

"What happened at the last university you taught at? Why did you leave?"

He had cooked me dinner, it was pasta, expertly done and we were sitting at the rickety brown table in his living room finishing a bottle of red wine. The candle melting in the old wine bottle sat between us. He looked at me for a while in silence, not a comfortable silence. His eyes were huge behind his glasses, they flickered blackly in the candlelight, and then he said carefully:

"There was a misunderstanding."

"What sort of misunderstanding?" I hardly dared to breathe. I felt like I was on the verge of a discovery. Instinct told me that it wouldn't be one that I necessarily wanted to make. But no. He took a gulp of wine and seemed to reconsider. The entire time he stared at my face, his eyes calm and empty.

"Nothing for you to worry about." He smiled with the greatest innocence, all boyish and preppy.

The next day I caught the train home for Christmas.

I had always loved the excitement and build-up to Christmas and there was something uniquely special about coming home that year. I guess that I felt a sense of achievement, even pride, that I was finally doing something normal. Time had passed, time was continuing to pass, and the nightmare in Mexico was becoming almost, not quite, but almost, a horrific event that had happened to someone else. My mum still wasn't home but my dad was manically, childishly, hopeful that she would soon return and obviously my presence meant that she was bound to visit often over Christmas. He was beyond excited.

"He's gone a bit loopy." said my brother dourly.

I almost didn't recognise my brother he had become so staid and humourless. His head was shaved military style and he wore sensible chinos and formal shirts as if he was an accountant in his forties.

"The girlfriend has made him like that." My mum told me sadly, "I think she tells him what to wear."

"Have you met her?"

"No, he won't let us!" she shrugged her shoulders ruefully.

It was midmorning and we were sitting in the living room with dad hovering obtrusively. I had arrived late the previous evening. My mum still looked elegant and trim and exquisitely made up. It seemed that the transformation was permanent and in no way dependant on the presence or absence of Jack in her life.

"Yes," my dad joined the conversation from the doorway, "I think he met her at some church group…"

"Church group? "asked my mum perplexed, "I'm sure he told me something else. You're looking well anyway, love!" she beamed at me, "Can't wait until you see what I bought you for Christmas!"

"Did you meet Caitlin at a church group?" I asked my brother.

"Not a church group, an actual church!" He sounded furious, "I met her in church! Did mum tell you to interrogate me?"

"I'm not interrogating you! Fuck! I'm just curious!"

"Can you not swear please, it's offensive."
"What? Oh sorry!" I was taken aback and I didn't know what to say to him. He had always been so laid back and we had never been religious.

"Does it make you happy?" I asked tentatively, afraid of getting my head bitten off.

He didn't seem happy. He looked like a man with worries, tense, old before his time.

"Of course," he turned away, his jaw rigid. "It provides me with structure."

I had no idea what to say to that.

"Anyway," he added, "She's coming over on Christmas Day, you'll meet her then."

"Do mum and dad know?"

"Not yet. I want to tell them but they're being so annoying about her!"

I stared at him with his solemn face and his super short hair,

"It's because you've changed." I said quietly.

"Changed? Me?" his voice cracked, he looked livid, "It was mum that left our family! I don't see anyone giving her a hard time!"

I actually agreed with him on some level but it was like conversing with an irate stranger, all remnants of my brother had evaporated.

Almost immediately after that chat, there was a knock at the door. I had retreated to my room to worry about my brother and my dad answered the door.

"Abs! It's for you!"

When I looked down the stairs and saw Ben in the doorway, I felt my heart sink, literally, my chest felt like it was dropping into my belly with a kind of sickly disappointment. Ben looked dreadful; emaciated and pale with fresh acne on his cheeks. He had never been this thin and his skin had never been this bad. I knew instantly, right then, that he was using heavily and not just pot. Dad gave me an uncomfortable look and I ushered Ben upstairs into my room. As soon as he got there, he leaned in to try and kiss me and he stank of old smoke and stale sweat and that musty fetid stench of damp, grubby clothes. I had just had a shower and I didn't want him anywhere near me.

"What's wrong?" he asked. His eyes were bloodshot and his lips were cracked. "You are still my girlfriend, right?"

I felt a slow dawning horror. Clearly what I had perceived as a gradual fizzing out of our relationship had not been interpreted in that way by Ben. I hadn't spoken to him on the phone for nearly a month by then. I had no idea what to say to him, but my confusion and consternation must have been written all over my face.

He sank onto the bed.

"Right." his eyes glared at me, hard.

"So, that's how it is." he nodded bleakly.

"I thought that you understood." I hung my head miserably.

"But you didn't tell me it was over! We didn't discuss it! How could I have understood anything?"

His voice was dark and bitter. Not loud, but full of malice. Suddenly, desperately, I wanted him out of my room and away from my clean things. I wanted him out of the house, he disgusted me. He must have read it in my face.

"Don't worry, I'm leaving!" he hissed, "Happy fucking Christmas!"

He stormed out of the room and down the stairs and I heard the door slam so loudly that vibrations resounded through the house. I stood at the window watching him jog away. A scrawny grey figure, his head down. I couldn't believe that I had ever been involved with him, my skin prickled with revulsion. He was so different from handsome James; they could have been a different species entirely.

"Alright love?" My dad stood in the doorway looking worried. In slippers, he looked older than he was. His shoulders were stooped and there were drooping bags under his eyes. I suddenly wanted to hug him but I didn't.

"Yeah, all Ok!" I forced myself to reply brightly, "Just a misunderstanding."

"He didn't look very well, that chap." my dad mused, raising an eyebrow at me but I just nodded in tacit agreement.

"You know who I saw in town the other day?" my dad continued in a jolly tone, obviously trying to cheer me up, "That Emma girl!"

"Emma?" my veins filled with ice

"You alright love?" Dad looked properly worried now. I felt dizzy, all the blood must have left my face.

"I thought that she was your mate? Didn't you hang out together in Mexico?"

My parents had never been told, by me or by anyone else, how Emma had deliberately left us in the desert.

"Ah, she was." I forced myself to breathe, "Not so much anymore."

"I think she goes to one of the fancy universities now, Oxford or Cambridge, one of those." Dad frowned in concentration; his brow furrowed.

I turned away so that he wouldn't see my face.

"Of course, she would, she was always really academic."

I squeezed my words out steadily. I felt like an actress forced to play a part with a gun pointing at her head. More than anything, I just wanted my dad to leave so that I could absorb all this.

"She was never beautiful like you though, hey love."

I wanted to cry but seemingly reassured that all was well, he finally left and I resumed staring out of the window, my mind churning, breathing deeply in and out, in and out. Of course, Emma would be here, back from her fancy university, on her Christmas break. It was nothing short of a miracle that I hadn't bumped into her sooner, before in the summer. She must have returned from Mexico at some point before starting university in September. It started hailing then, freezing globs of ice fell on the dead squares of tiny suburban garden. The sky was a heavy dark grey. I suddenly wished that I was back in Penbridge, far from my town and far from the malevolent phantoms of Ben and Emma.

Chapter 27

Christmas day dawned wet and rainy. The hail of the previous week had transformed briefly into slushy snow but that had only lasted a day or two. I watched the brief, miraculous white landscape from my window. I didn't leave the house. I hadn't left it since Ben's visit, not even for a walk. Dad was too distracted by the imminent Christmas celebrations and, more precisely, the prospect of seeing mum, to realise and be concerned.

She arrived early that day. I could hear my dad's over-excited greeting at the front door and feel the trickle of frozen air leak into the house. I knew that I should head downstairs, make an effort to contribute to the festive spirit but I felt rooted to the floor. Increasingly, I felt bound by the heaviness of this inertia. An exhaustion so deep that it seemed to reside in my very bones. Then the doorbell rang again and I heard the boom of my dad's greeting and the thin tinkle of a girl's voice. I knew that this must be Caitlin and my curiosity finally propelled me down the stairs to see the creature who had turned my brother religious.

My mum, dad, Caitlin and my brother were all sitting around the Christmas tree in the living room when I walked in, like bad actors on the set of a Christmas commercial. Everyone was wearing a garish Christmas jumper except for my mum (I was still in my pyjamas) and everyone, including my mum, was sporting a wide grin which looked phony even if it wasn't. There were too many teeth on display. Caitlin was a tall, thin, pale girl with a severe bob and fringe, wearing a pink fluffy jumper which made her look sickly. Her features were tiny. She wasn't attractive and this offended my sensibilities in some deep primal way which I couldn't admit, even to myself. We were a good-looking family. My brother was handsome. I'd have expected his girlfriend to be at least pretty. I would never have voiced those thoughts out loud, even to myself.

She was very well-mannered and polite. She didn't seem remotely nervous at spending Christmas day in a strange home. She was weirdly self-assured and my brother fawned all over her like a fool. It was disturbing to watch. I could tell that it bothered my mum too. She kept catching my eye and raising her eyebrows and giving me these odd twisty half-smiles. My dad was so thoroughly delighted to have my mum there, that nothing bothered him in the slightest. He looked like a man who had just won the lottery.

We sat down in the living room and opened the gifts. Caitlin also having received generic-type presents from all of us, of course. My mum gave me a small wrapped box. It was a bit bigger than a jewellery box but I still presumed it held a bangle or something similar. Instead, I was shocked and amazed to find some car keys. Everyone stopped opening their own presents and stared. We were not the type of people (wealthy) who would blithely gift cars for Christmas.

"What?" shrugged mum, feigning indifference "Don't look at me like that! It's just second hand!"

Then, giggly and excited like kids going on a trip, we put on our shoes and coats and went to look at it. I still had my pyjamas on and it had started to snow lightly again.

This is one of my favourite memories, still now.

The whole thing felt silly as if we were already a bit drunk. Only Caitlin remained po-faced and I didn't care. It was a tiny car, immaculately clean. I knew nothing about cars but appreciated the significance of owning one, both the generosity of the gift and the freedom it bestowed on me. The thought came to me unbidden; so that's how money makes people happy. Then hilarity arrived, Caitlin's sombre face and my brother trying not to smile. All of it jealousy disguised as righteousness, I thought. Simon said;

"You know that's way too much for a Christmas present." in a disapproving tome and I stuck my tongue out at him. Caitlin saw me and her eyes widened. I was desperate to say something about having a poker up their arses but I restrained myself. I even got dressed into proper clothes. The very idea of the car, the fact of it belonging to me made me undeniably happy. Christmas day was therefore a success for me and my dad. Definitely. My mum looked pleased too. although I could tell that she was anxious about my brother's relationship with Caitlin. The two of them looked tense all the time. All day, I never saw them relax and smile naturally. A small, evil part of me thought of slipping a vodka shot into their orange juice but, of course, I didn't.

Caitlin left mid-afternoon whilst we were all slouching round the TV drinking Baileys and eating chocolate. My brother saw her out and then came back into the living room and announced vehemently;

"I know you all have something to say but don't, Ok? I don't want to hear it!"

Then he stomped up the stairs to his room like a stroppy kid.

In that instant, overfed and drunk, it all felt so ridiculous that we looked at each other and burst out laughing.

There was a deflation in spirits after Christmas day as there always is. A Christmas card arrived from Penny in Mexico, a generic card which showed a Santa and said Happy Christmas and 'love Penny'. There was no personal message. I felt bad as I hadn't sent her one. I hadn't sent any cards at all. I started thinking about her. Inevitably, I remembered her in the desert and the way it felt. How our throats felt gritty like sandpaper. I would start thinking about things and then I couldn't stop, my brain wouldn't stop tormenting me.

My brother was always out, I presumed with Caitlin, and I was always in. I didn't want to risk bumping into Ben, or indeed the rest of the gang. Above all, I didn't want to bump into Emma. My mum was hanging out at our house every morning for a cup of tea and my dad was on a massive high. It was painful to watch. It was obvious that he was sure that she would return to him and yet to me, it was not obvious at all. I got the impression that she was relishing her independence and I doubted that she would willingly relinquish it again, even for him.

"It's a shame," mused mum one morning, "that you can't get your job back in that restaurant, it's always good to have a job, that extra bit of money, you know. You never know when it may come in handy…"

I felt far more sympathy for her now that I knew about her past, but the thought of walking back into that restaurant turned my stomach.

"I just can't, mum, I can't work with Ben and the others again, it would just get nasty."

"You'll have to start getting over stuff like that you know."

She was right. Now, should I need a job, which I undoubtably would, I'd have to go through the whole rigmarole of finding another one.

"What about your other friends? Don't you want to see them?"

Every day, mum seemed to get a bit more inquisitive as if she'd set herself the task of finding out as much as possible about me before I headed back to Uni. I started counting down the days until I could realistically return. The only time I left the house was for 'driving lessons' with my dad in my new car. I had learnt to drive and passed my test when I was seventeen but hadn't driven since then. That half an hour a day felt like a bonding experience. My dad had grown quite portly with a wide girth and the car was petite. Us both sitting in it and driving it around the block made me think of a child's cartoon. My happiness with my car remained undiminished and I tried to hold it in the forefront of my mind. On the edges, were other grey things which I tried not to dwell on.

Dad was worried about me driving all the way up to Penbridge on my own. He announced that he would take his own car and follow me all the way up in case I ran into difficulties. This felt unnecessary to me and I didn't appreciate it then. I didn't appreciate any of the things which he did for me. Now, I appreciate them. Now that it is too late.

We had a quiet New Year's Eve at home, just me, mum and dad. Simon had gone to Caitlin's house about which we were all relieved. We didn't discuss it but I knew that none of us liked her, she made us uncomfortable. Mum kept asking if I was sure I wouldn't rather be hanging out with my friends instead. It was touching, how popular she thought I was. I didn't understand why she thought I had any friends left there. Perhaps, it was just wishful thinking.

On the second of January, in a light freezing drizzle, I drove back to Penbridge with my dad trailing behind me in his car. We went slowly and it took us a good long while. I would glimpse him in my rear-view mirror, his kind serious face deep in concentration. We pulled in to a bland service station enroute, and sat at a plastic table drinking bad coffee. I felt a great fondness for him in my heart, which, again, I should have acknowledged at the time, but didn't.

By the time we pulled into the car park in Penbridge, the sun was setting and it felt as if we had arrived in another country. The grand majestic setting streaked with pink light, the ancient trees, the tiny insignificant people beneath all that endless sky.

I insisted that my dad came in and had a cup of tea and something to eat before heading back and prayed that one of the others had brought supplies. Both Carrie and Julian were sitting at the kitchen table as if they had never left and then I remembered that they actually hadn't left. Neither of them had gone home for Christmas. Carrie because it was too far and because she wanted to stay away from the reminders of Casey, and Julian because he had told me, very simply, that he didn't want to. They looked so cosy and comfortable sitting there and the thought crossed my mind that there may be something between them. They were very welcoming to both me and dad and I felt in that instant like another happier person.

However, I knew, even then, that it wouldn't last. There was no evidence immediately available to back that feeling, it was just there, set in stone. Dad was his usual friendly self and we all had an amiable chat and cup of tea. He always had a misguided respect for college kids. He, himself, had never been to university and I knew that this was because he had never had the opportunity. However, he always made out that it was simply because he wasn't clever enough. It was an untruth that he clung to, despite all evidence to the contrary. Anyway, he made Carrie and Julian feel important in the way that he addressed them. Knowing the empty spaces in their self-esteem as I did, this was probably no bad thing.

By the time he left, we had had enough of tea and moved onto wine. Deedee returned like a whirlwind, her hair now straightened and dyed blue. A storm seemed to be brewing outside, a vicious wind howled. Just outside the kitchen window, all the bins had been knocked over and were rolling around clattering against each other. Fortunately, they were still empty. It felt snug in the kitchen. There was the ubiquitous melted candle in a bottle on the table, someone's lava lamp in the corner casting strange blue patterns on our faces, the musty fug of our cigarettes and the cheap acidic wine, combined. Right then and there, these were the people that I felt most comfortable with.

Chapter 28

I had a lecture with James on the following day. It was in one of the bigger lecture halls and he didn't pay me any attention during the class, he didn't even look at me. I was baffled. What the hell was wrong with him? I stared at him fixedly, to the point where I was sure that the others would notice, but still he blanked me. Who was I kidding, gossip was rife, had been rife for a long time. After the lecture, I stayed in my seat pretending to fiddle with my stuff whilst the others filed out. I acted as if I'd lost something under my chair. When I extracted my head, he was still at the lectern but staring right at me with a cold, grim look on his face. I felt myself blanche. He had never looked at me like that before. Sometimes, he was a bit unfriendly but this was something else.

"Forget all about me, did you?" he growled in a low furious voice.

He was still standing behind the lectern. He looked, in that instant, nasty.

"What do you mean?" I stammered, scrambling to my feet.

"Didn't bother to get in touch, did you? All Christmas? Do you think I'm just here for your convenience?"

I was baffled. I had no idea what to say. He hadn't mentioned anything about keeping in touch before the holidays. I'd presumed that he hadn't wanted to, that he wanted to maintain the utmost secrecy. I had his number at the cottage but he had firmly given me to understand that I was only to use it in an absolute emergency.

"I WAS HERE!" he bellowed, banging his fist down on his notes, "I WAS HERE WAITING!"

I looked around but there was no one about. The door had slammed shut after the last student. I felt fear then. My body felt it first, a weakness in the legs, a dip in the stomach, an uncontrollable trembling in the fingers. Fight or flight, I thought, but in that instant, I forgot what it meant. I stood stock still, not trusting myself to move and he left. I heard his furious footsteps echo down the corridor. I went back to my room. I was too shocked to hang out with the others, to rearrange my features into a socially acceptable expression. I lay flat on my back on my bed, smoking and staring at the institutional ceiling; ugly cream coloured plastic tiles with tiny grey spots. A bit later Deedee banged on my door and I joined her for dinner and pretended to be normal. I felt a lump in my throat the entire time as if something was stuck there and I couldn't swallow it down.

The next day, I was returning from another lecture alone on the interminable path. There were students whom I knew ahead of me and behind me but I didn't feel like talking to anyone. It was an oddly warm day and I felt my red wool scarf itch and prickle against my skin. Seemingly out of nowhere, James suddenly materialised by my side. He was panting as if he'd been running. His face was flushed and looked swollen and bruised. I peered at him curiously and recognised that the puffy look was the after effect of tears. I kept walking, my head down, breathing into my scarf.

"I'm so sorry!" he gasped, still out of breath, "I don't know what came over me. I missed you so much, it was so lonely in that cottage. Day after day, alone, you know? I think that after a while, I lost perspective, went a bit mad. I didn't mean to scare you, I'm so, so sorry!"

A tiny rebellious voice in my head hissed into my ear: If he had really wanted to, he could have found my number in some university database. They had my parents' details. Unfortunately,

I was not rebellious enough, however. I melted. I gave in. He grovelled and I acquiesced. We separated so as not to be observed and via different routes we ended up back at the caretaker's cottage.

The next day, in the supermarket with Julian, whilst we were trying to rip open the plastic covering on small cartons of juice, I saw Dylan looming.

"Fuck!" muttered Julian. He grabbed my hand and physically dragged me down the aisle and out of the 'in' door. Our basket sat abandoned next to the juices. It was drizzling and we ran. We could have stopped, of course, Dylan was not behind us, he hadn't even left the supermarket. But we didn't stop. Only outside our accommodation block did we bend over gasping, Julian retching. He looked very purple of face.

"Just unfit." he mumbled, dismissing my concerns.

Once inside, I tried to get him to talk to me about Dylan but he wouldn't. He kept saying;

"Story for another day. Don't push me!" But I wouldn't, couldn't stop badgering him. Probably because I needed the distraction from my own demons. I went on and on and finally, he sighed, slumped at the kitchen table, he actually sat up and banged his two large fists against it and I jumped, startled, my heckles raised, and then I calmed my breathing right down and took a deep breath. It was only Julian.

"If I tell you, will you leave it alone? Never talk about it again?"

"Yes, yes, sure."

"I mean it…seriously? Also, you are not to tell the others! I don't want them to pity me any more than they already do."

"What are you on about? They don't pity you! Why would they?" I laughed nervously because it was a lie. They probably did pity him and his obvious sadness.

"Whatever." He stood up wearily and filled the kettle. We both waited in silence as steam filled the room and it started whistling. In front of our kitchen window, a ferrety-looking boy student was putting his bin bag in one of the communal bins. We always had to have the windows shut because of the stench.

"So," Julian began, "I told you that we went to school together, Dylan and I, and that we were friends."

"Oh, I kind of thought you weren't friends, he said you were but…"

"Would you let me speak!" he glared at me exasperated. I nodded, "Sorry." I muttered.

"It was a small town, still is, we were together in primary school and then together again in secondary school. We were friends because we were both into music and, well, there wasn't that many kids into music, barely any. I was more interested in classical always, even as a small kid, which was unusual and not in a good way. We weren't in London or in any other big, sophisticated city! Our parents weren't educated, well mine are teachers so mine were, more than most…but my point is that we didn't live in some cultured hub where a fat boy playing classical music on the piano would be appreciated."

"Wow. I didn't realise that you play the piano!"

"I play everything really, most instruments, but when I was a kid, it was pretty much just the piano."

"OK, so didn't you want to just focus on that and become some…I don't know…child prodigy or something?"

"I just told you!" he snapped, "It just got me bullied, fat and piano playing, it was not a good look!"

"Oh sorry." I cowered almost, surprised at his temper.

"No," he sighed, "I'm sorry, I didn't mean to snap at you. It's him, being here, it just reminds me of literally everything that I want to forget."

"I know exactly what you mean." I said with feeling, thinking, with a shudder, of that shock of yellow hair continuously cropping up unexpectedly and always making my heart jolt.

"Anyway, we were friends, great friends actually in primary. He was literally the only other piano player, although, to be fair, and, I don't mean to brag, I was far better… he was already, even when he was ten, starting to make noises about being a rock star, guitar players were considered cool, bass guitar especially, so he persuaded his parents to get him one of those…"

"Oh yeah, I remember." I thought back to my own parochial school, all the supposedly cool girls hankering after the bass guitar players of the popular bands.

He went to put the kettle on again. The room felt cosy, outside the rain hammered down again and battered against the windows. Wordlessly, he refilled my mug and carried on;

"He wasn't much good at the guitar, to be honest, or at the singing lessons, which he also persuaded his parents to pay for. He should have just stuck to piano like me, he was, I always suspected, a bit of a one trick pony. But, unfortunately for everyone, he wasn't having any of it. As soon as we got to secondary school, he was running around trying to get a band together. It was embarrassing. He was a skinny little squirt and I was, still, his fat friend, and he kept trying to persuade these big, super-cool boys to start a band with us…I, personally, also didn't want anything to do with this hypothetical band, but I was shy and awkward and intimidated in that school and he was my only friend and I felt as if I had to stick with him…"

"For years," he carried on, "Everyone ignored him, and he kind of grudgingly stuck with me. I never became cool in any way, I knew that there was no point even trying to pretend…I was still playing the piano back then, but Dylan, well, Dylan, to give him credit, practised really hard and did get better at his guitar, I mean, he practised for hours and hours every night, a monkey would have been able to play well, the amount of time he put into it and then…finally…at the age of about fourteen, fifteen he managed to form a band. He had grown by then too, become tall. I don't know if he was attractive…"

"He's definitely not attractive, no." I shook my head emphatically.

"But… he was, if not exactly talented, just talented enough, to play in this band he put together with a few of the older boys. It was a kind of New Romantic, rock combo. The other boys in the band were twins. They were extremely handsome. Italian or half-Italian, I don't recall, but mean. People considered them to be funny and mean, but to me they were just mean. I don't know if they had a word to Dylan about me, how I was bad for their image or whatever, but from one day to the next, he dropped me as a friend. That was bad enough. I was now totally alone, all day every day, being fat and lonely, but that wasn't even it…To this day, I don't know why, what compelled them, but both Dylan and his new friends the twins, they were called Dino and Dario, they made my life fucking miserable…"

Julian went red. I saw his eyes filling with tears which he tried to blink back. He rubbed one large hand nervously against the other forearm. I remembered, in that instant, exactly how it felt, all of it.

"Fucking miserable." he reiterated, "I mean physically, just the name calling, I was used to that, I could cope with that. Sticks and stones and the rest of it…but there were actually, real sticks and stones, that was the thing…and I was so stupid, I couldn't even get my head around it, I mean, he was my friend! You know, that's what I thought! What a fucking idiot I was!"

"What did they do? I mean…if you want to tell me…"

"In the school itself, just petty stuff, you know, they couldn't risk getting into trouble, the twins especially were already on a black list somewhere, I'm sure…They would wait until I was just about to go through a door and then slam it in my face, or trip me up whenever they could get close to me. As you can imagine, I would avoid them like the plague. I used to sit next to Dylan in class, but he moved himself away from me and I ended up sitting alone right in front of the teacher. To be honest, miserable as that was, I was glad as time passed. At least, whilst I was there, I was protected. Dylan took a while to warm up to the physical bullying…he seemed to be reluctant at first. Who knows why…maybe some vestige of decency remained, but, in any case, he was fully aware of what his new friends were doing and didn't prevent it and as time went on, he not only endorsed it, but joined in."

At that point, the kitchen door opened and we both started. I was so heavily involved in his story, that I had almost forgotten where we were. It was Dee.

"Oh, sorry guys! You look startled! Didn't mean to interrupt, I'll leave you to it…do you mind if I just, very quickly, make myself a coffee?"

She looked from one to the other of us puzzled and a bit disconcerted. I struggled to smile to reassure her and she smiled back, seemingly appeased.

"Won't be a minute!" she bustled about cheerfully, seemingly not minding the heavy silence that she was moving around in.

Once she had left, and shut the door quietly, Julien carried on.

"They knew my route home and they would wait for me, ambush me, if you will. It was a busy route, it wasn't as if I was walking across woodland or going down little alleyways, none of that, I wasn't stupid. It was all just dull residential roads and there were always people about! Mums picking younger kids up, older kids in clusters. They didn't even care. As I said, first it would just be the twins but then Dylan would join in, tentatively at first but then he started to enjoy himself, I could tell, blood lust, that's what it was. They would just wait behind a bush or a fence and then jump out and push me down onto the pavement and kick the shit out of me. I tried leaving school later or earlier. I tried varying my route, but sooner or later they would always cotton on and it would happen again. Often, other people saw. Mostly, they would watch from a distance. If it was older school kids, they would watch with a kind of gleeful fascination. Mums would bustle their younger kids away as soon as they could. Occasionally, some older bloke would try to intervene and even more occasionally, it would work and they would run off. However, they were big the twins, as well as being 'musicians', they used to go to the gym a lot…Dino especially was built like a brick shithouse."

He removed a crumpled cigarette packet from the pocket of his jeans and offered me one. I noticed his hands were trembling. I took the lighter from him and lit the cigarettes. We sat there smoking in silence for some time. It had stopped raining but the sky was grey and overcast. We did not put a light on but sat in the gloomy warm fug.

"It went on for many years." Julian carried on, "I'm sure people knew. I tried to disguise all the injuries from my parents, but they must have known. I don't think anything was ever actually broken but I was in pain and limping all the time. They stomped on my fingers and for about six months I couldn't play the piano at all. Even now, two of my fingers are twisted and deformed."

Reflexively, I looked at his hand holding the cigarette, and it was true, his two middle fingers had an odd slant about them. How had I not noticed that before?

"What bothered me the most…" his fist closed round the cigarette, he could have been powerful with the right backing, I saw that now, but it wasn't in him.

"What bothered me the most is that people knew and did nothing. My bloody parents knew and did nothing…in my head…I just can't reconcile that…it doesn't make any sense to me. It was sort of true, of course you grew up at the same time…sort of true, that everyone was expected to be tough, that was the mantra where I lived anyway, put up and shut up, all that crap…anyway…"

"Did they all go to sixth form then?"

"No, Dylan did, I know, but the twins were thick, they left, but in any case, I was out of there as fast as my fat legs would carry me! I went to a sixth form college miles away, just to get as far away as possible…you can imagine my horror when I saw him here, in the fucking music department no less and then he keeps hassling you as well, I mean, what the actual fuck…"

"I didn't realise, I'm so sorry, and that you have to see him every day as well…"

"Fortunately, the music department is huge, I try and steer clear…also I hear that he is struggling so with any luck he'll fail his end of year exams and get kicked out."

I didn't know what to say. There was nothing much to say. We smoked together in the half-light and I patted his hand.

I was trying to be comforting.

The days got longer. The furious weather abated a bit. After that weird outburst at the beginning of January, James acted normal, even sweet on occasion, sometimes cloyingly sweet and clingy. He wanted me to spend all my time with him. He never wanted me to go to the bar, for instance.

Deedee snorted. "Doesn't 'allow' you to go? Seriously?"

"It's not like that." I mumbled, not sure whether it was like that or not. It was certainly easier to give in than to argue and at the back of my mind was the suppressed memory of his rage. It was a monster who I would do anything not to be reacquainted with. Also, our outings to the bar were always beset with anxiety for me, fear of running into either Zoe or Dylan. It wasn't that much of a sacrifice not to go.

Furthermore, there was the work. It was easier for some people than for others and I was clearly one of the weaker students. Too much pot smoking maybe, all those drugs had befuddled my brain. In any case, I had to work hard. I put in the hours, in the library and in my room. I'd get headaches from forgetting to drink and Deedee or Julian would take turns banging on my door to remind me that I needed a cup of tea and a break. Carrie was the only person that I knew who worked harder than me and she was rarely home. She spent long hours in the hospital in addition to the lengthy lectures and stints in the library. She looked drawn and exhausted and tinier than ever.

In late March a tentative Spring blossomed. Everyone felt instantly lighter and more cheerful, it was as if a murky weight had lifted. The campus was lush and verdant and wild flowers sprang up in joyful clumps in unexpected places. We finally shelved our heavy coats, our scarves and gloves and probably for the first time, truly appreciated our rural surroundings.

Deedee suggested going for a walk by the river.

"The river?" I had always found something creepy about the existence of the river. It was like a phantom, unseen and possibly malevolent.

"Sure, apparently it's just a short walk through the woods." She shrugged

"Hmm…" I was sceptical, "Ok, but let's get the others to come too" I was firmly convinced then, correctly as it turned out, that there was safety in numbers.

So, on one rarely beautiful Sunday morning, when the sky was a calm translucent blue, we packed some sandwiches and a few snacks, a ramshackle picnic, and set off to explore. Deedee, the most sociable and gregarious one, had asked around and found out that there was no official track leading from the main path to the river. You just had to make your own way through the woods. We could, in theory, have entered the woods from directly behind our accommodation block but we chose, instead, to deviate from the path leading to the student bar. That was the place where we always became glaringly aware of the presence of the river, the spot where we heard it calling to us.

The woods were as dense as they looked. It felt like we had revisited the gloom of winter, meagre light entered and the sky was barely visible. We had to concentrate hard on where to put our feet in the packed foliage, in case we tripped. There were hidden tree roots everywhere. It wasn't a pleasant walk and at times panic set in and I wanted to give up, but the others were oblivious and cheerful. Even Julian, large and sweaty, was shouldering on determinedly. I felt ashamed of my weakness and I didn't want to let them down. They already saw me as a wimp. About fifteen minutes later, we arrived at the river. It was narrower than I thought that it would be, about 50 metres across, but it was aggressive. It hurtled over rocks and stones, gushing thunderously. Close up, it was, of course, much louder. We had to raise our voices. We all stood and stared at it for a while, transfixed.

"Wow!" exclaimed Deedee

"Wow, indeed" said Julian, panting, "Shall we have our sandwiches now?"

Behind us, the trees seemed to close up again, obliterating any trace of our presence. Carrie turned to me. She looked like a child hiking with her parents, so insignificant and tiny, those huge trees framing her like ogres.

"Are you alright?" she asked me, "You're a bit pale?"

"I'm fine." I retorted brusquely

"Oh, ok!" she laughed lightly, "I'm just practising my doctoring skills!"

There was a path running along the side of the river which was wide enough for three people. It was all gravel and stones. We walked along it, on Julian's insistence, chewing on our sandwiches. I was glad to see the sky again and forced myself to relax. It was just a spring walk with friends after all, there was nothing here to fear.

Chapter 29

After that, as the days got longer still and the weather warmer, we went walking that way more often. It became familiar. I no longer thought of the river as an ominous presence. In the bright light, it appeared cheerful and bubbly, like a chatty friend.

I was walking down the path by the river with Deedee one Sunday in April. None of us had gone home for Easter break. We had exams directly after and needed access to the library. I hadn't been home since Christmas. Subconsciously, I guess that I didn't want to run into Ben and Emma. Nothing further had happened with my parents. I got updates every week, all three of my close family providing me with a slightly different version of events. From what I could gather, my dad still hoped and my mum still dashed his hopes to the ground. They both beseeched me to come back. My dad because he missed me and wanted an ally, and my mum because she wanted help in extricating Simon from the clutches of Caitlin. They were showing no signs of splitting up, on the contrary, my mum was terrified that they were going to get engaged. My brother was studying for his A-levels.

"Don't be silly!" I tried to reassure her, "Surely, Simon will go to University."

"I think she's trying to persuade him to tie the knot before."

"That's ridiculous!" I said firmly, but I remembered the rigid set of Caitlin's jaw and her humourless expression and I was worried too.

Anyway, that day by the river, I was trying to relax. I had so much work to get through that I felt panicky and overwhelmed. I was trying to organise it all in my head, trying to work out how I could dedicate the necessary hours to the various subjects before the exams and still get some sleep. Deedee was telling me that I worried too much. She was quite glib about her studies and she didn't get stressed. Chiefly because she didn't need to. She complained that the work was hard and yet she always got top marks. I never did.

Anyway, we were deep in thought and conversation, nearly oblivious to our surroundings, when suddenly, from directly behind us we heard the loud crack of wood breaking, a large twig, perhaps a small branch. We both swung our heads round. My heart pounded maniacally and cold sweat drenched me. I was always a hair trigger away from pure fear. We couldn't see anything. I couldn't see anything yet I was still convinced that there was something there. Behind us were just the secretive rustling trees but then Deedee grabbed my arm. We were still squinting into the shadows.

"Didn't you see it?" she shrieked

"What?" my mouth went dry. If she had seen something too, then it wasn't just something conjured up by my own imagination.

"Something yellow!" she laughed, "Something bright yellow, a yellow bear!" she started giggling hysterically but I stared at her. For her, this wasn't serious, for me it was.

"Really? Are you making this up?"

"Chill! For God's sake! There's nothing there!"

"But really? Did you see something yellow?"

"I think so, but it could have been anything! A leaf? A petal?"

"There are no petals in the wood." I told her grimly, "No bright flowers."

"How do you know?"

She was right. I didn't know for sure.

"You have to chill." She laid her hand on my arm again, but I couldn't calm down. At the forefront of my mind was the image of Zoe's hair bopping about through the trees. Was she following me? If so, what for? What did she want from me?

I was still feeling jumpy the next day when, on exiting my accommodation block, I noticed a lanky figure to the side, just hovering. To my horror, I realised that it was Dylan. After my conversation with Julian, I was more afraid of him than before. Now I knew what he was capable of. Defence is the best form of attack, I remembered. I forced my breathing to still and shoved my trembling hands into my pockets.

"What do you want?" I demanded. He had walked towards me and looked over-excited, a bit frantic, like an eager dog. He always looked a bit like that with me, but I pictured him, with the safe backing of a gang, as a predator.

"I need to tell you something." he started.

"NO!" I practically shouted, having tried to adopt my most authoritative voice

"NO! You don't need to tell me anything!"

"HE HAD AN AFFAIR WITH A STUDENT AND HE BEAT HER UP, THAT'S WHY HE WAS KICKED OUT!"

He shouted all this, his words all ran together. It took a second before I could absorb what he meant. He was so determined that I didn't get away before he could tell me what he had come to say. Why? I didn't understand. What did he have against James or against me? Was he threatened by either of us or by both? Was he obsessed by me? Was it something to do with Julian? I never found out. He kept shouting but the words seemed garbled, there was a lot of swearing. All around, people across vast distances were turning to stare. Out of the corner of my eye, through the glass pane in the door of the accommodation block, I could see a girl frozen on the stairs, not wanting to interrupt whatever unpleasant scene this was, just standing there waiting. I needed him to get away from me. More than anything else, I needed to be as far away from him as possible. I felt his revolting presence crawl on my skin. I shoved him, hard. By now, with the ranting, he was that close, an arm's width away. Then I ran, I didn't stop to see him fall. I ran as fast as I could, away from him down the path and he didn't follow.

James didn't deny any of it when I went to see him, shaken and confused, in the caretaker's cottage that evening. He lit a candle, as he always did for me. He believed that I liked all the romantic cliches, which was probably true then. I wanted to believe in him. That was the main issue. I had become dependent on his feelings for me as if I was in some way validated by them. He poured me a glass of wine and we sat at the rickety table in the cluttered living room. The flame danced on his handsome face and he looked strangely relaxed considering the torrid accusations that I had just thrown at him.

"So." he smiled, a bit condescendingly, as if I was a student who needed calming down, which I was in a way.

"Let me get this straight. Some creepy guy who probably fancies you, who's been following you about for ages, comes to you with this totally mad, trumped up, cock and bull story, and you believe him?"

His tone, which had started off calm and quiet, got progressively louder and increasingly irate. I felt my stomach clench in warning. There was no longer amusement in his eyes but something colder and darker. Without preamble, his fist came down hard onto the table and the candle in its bottle leapt up, landed on its side and went out. In the sudden semi-darkness, I jumped up and headed straight towards the door but he was quicker than me. Taller and stronger and the bulk of his body blocked my exit. He gripped my upper arms as if he was about to lift me up and shake me. His fingers dug into my muscles and I cried out.

"If I let you go," his voice echoed in the grey light, stern, emotionless and chilling, "You will not run." My arms throbbed with pain. "No!" I whimpered.

He led me back to the table and we sat again and I tried not to let him read my face, I was shaking. I stared at the candle which he had put back and lit as if by doing this order would be restored. I tried to get my mind to work but it was panicked and frozen. How could I get away? How long would I be kept here? Why was this happening to me again? He kept talking in a low threatening rumble, a series of admonishments and warnings. The candle light flickered on his face and I realised for the first time, that there was a cruelty in it. How had I not noticed before? After some time, he mellowed. His voice and face softened and he wanted to take me to bed and I let him. I didn't feel as if I had a choice.

Afterwards, I didn't sleep. I lay there quietly all night, barely breathing so that I wouldn't disturb him. I was too scared to run into the dark. He slept deeply and in repose looked blameless and insipidly handsome now, the cruelty erased. As soon as the first light seeped into the room and the birds started chirping, I gathered my stuff together very slowly and quietly, and left the cottage. There was no one about, it was obscenely beautiful, the birds were calling each other merrily, in any other circumstances it would have been idyllic. As it was, I ran and ran through the silence, intent on escaping the encroaching danger.

I pretended that I was sick. I told my teachers that I had flu, a really bad dose which wouldn't let up. I hung around the flat listlessly. My teachers sent me work which I struggled to focus on and did half-heartedly. James didn't send anything. I knew that my flatmates were worried and I tried to act normal around them. The days got sunnier and more beautiful as if mocking me. I stared out of the kitchen window at the bins. Beyond that sad tableau, kids like me were having fun, I knew. They were tanned and healthy and sociable, having picnics and barbecues and forming lifelong friendships. Summer was the best time of year here but apparently, none of that was for me. Deedee and Julian tried to force me out every day, even just to the shop for a walk, but I wouldn't go. I couldn't sleep. I lay on my back with my eyes wide open. There was darkness outside and darkness within. I imagined I heard predators outside my window. I kept it locked with the curtains drawn.

"This has to stop!" Deedee came to my room one day and stood in the middle of the floor, shouting angrily.

"If you don't go to lectures you will fail, and then what will happen?"

"I don't know" I answered miserably. But she was right, of course. If I failed, my life would be even more of a mess. I agreed to leave the flat on the unofficial proviso that I would always be accompanied by someone, like an invalid. My flatmates seemed to know, instinctively, that this was the deal. Carrie couldn't help as she was always too busy but Deedee and Julian were always with me, loyal babysitters. It reminded me of when I returned from Mexico. There were baby steps to start with and then strength and confidence increased gradually. Obviously, I did not attend James's lectures anymore but managed to get the notes from another student. I also requested a change of tutor which was granted, unchallenged and unquestioned. This surprised me and then I wondered about that. Maybe they knew, I thought. Maybe they all knew. Maybe they'd known about him all along. Maybe I was the only ignorant one.

Chapter 30

It was June and I was getting on with it. There were exams and I was barely scraping through them, but it was better than failing completely. Just a pass meant that I could return the following year. I still didn't spend much time outside but on the odd occasion, I went, accompanied of course, on a walk or to the supermarket as well as to all my lectures except those taught by James.

Once, at the supermarket, I saw him. I was putting bananas into a paper bag and I felt, even before I saw, someone edge closer to me. I instantly froze. Panic set in immediately. I couldn't even turn my head to see where Julian was.

"Don't worry." said James in a very low, controlled voice. He lay both hands before him as if to demonstrate that he was unarmed. They looked tanned, his fingers, slim. Something whimpered in me.

"You'll be glad to hear that I'm leaving at the end of term."

"OK." I whispered and that was all. It was as if he was setting me free.

I carried on standing there alone, the bananas dangling from my hand stupidly. People veered around me as if I was an obstacle. When, finally, Julian came to find me, he said, "Abs, it's OK." and put his arm around me. We paid for our shopping and went home. I felt safer after that somehow. Now that I knew that he was leaving, I was fairly sure that he would no longer approach me. I relaxed more. I felt my lungs widen, the perpetual lump in my throat ease up. Occasionally, I even went on a walk on my own. But I wasn't carefree like the others, of course not, not like I should have been. Somewhere in the part of my brain which wasn't befuddled by anxiety, I resented that.

To celebrate Deedee's birthday at the end of June, I agreed to go to the bar. I hadn't been for so long that I was even looking forward to it. I put on clean jeans, a vest top as the weather was really warm and the tiniest bit of make-up. I had lost weight. The jeans gaped around my waist and hung baggily over my hips. I looked far paler than everyone else. I no longer thought of myself as beautiful. Nevertheless, I was determined, in that instant to go to the bar with my friends, to be a normal student. To at least act as if I was a normal student.

The four of us set out together in a jovial mood and sat at our favourite table on the outer edges, away from the raucous sporty gangs who congregated, as always, around the bar itself. I started to get a bit drunk, we were drinking sparkling wine in honour of Dee's birthday, and I felt myself relax. I let myself get giggly and silly. We sang along to the music and put our arms around each other. I didn't ever go to the bar, the others would do that for me, it was an unspoken agreement. I didn't even look in that direction. As the night wore on, we started doing tequila shots. I was getting too drunk. I could feel it; that slow-dawning stupidity of every intoxicated person who knows that they've taken it too far. I could see myself reflected in the glazed eyes and sloppy, jerky gestures of the others. It was time to go. I said that I wanted to go and they agreed. Their concern and protectiveness over me dominated every outing. I didn't appreciate them enough. I had that thought then, it was very clear. I was overcome with sentimental affection.

It was on the way out that I saw them. I was first. We were elbowing our way through the crowd trying to get to the exit. It was packed as usual and they were all drunk. It was like trying to push your way through a swaying forest. Suddenly, shockingly, to the left of me and part of a group of massive rugby boys, I spotted both Zoe and Paul. I stared at both of them, my eyes dancing, blurring, horrified, moving from one to the other. So similar and so sinister, those bland moon faces and bright yellow hair. They didn't see me, I didn't think that they had seen me but I ran, or tried to, shoving people recklessly out of the way. I presumed that my friends were right behind me. Once outside, I started running properly. The hazy summer light still clung on but the campus was empty and still, swathed in shadows.

As I ran, the music receded and the woodland sounds came at me from all angles. The rustling and murmuring of wind through leaves, the haunting calls of unseen birds. I looked around and realised that the others were too far behind me and that I was very alone. I slowed to a walk which was probably quite wobbly. I felt a bit panicked, drunk and sick.

Suddenly, out of nowhere, I felt a sharp pain to the back of my head. Before I could react, it happened again. I couldn't process what was happening. I fell to the ground and then there was a period of nothing, I must have passed out. Sometime later, crawling out of a sticky confused sleep, I opened my eyes to see my friends standing around me. My head hurt. Deedee was crying and Carrie was screaming "Someone call 911!" Julian was panting, his face red, he had his arm round her and he kept repeating "No 999! We need to call 999, Carrie 911 is the States!" In spite of everything I smiled and they all peered down at me, their faces so close that I could touch them.

"She's OK!" shouted Deedee, and then I must have passed out again.

The next time I opened my eyes, I was being loaded onto a stretcher and an oxygen mask was being lowered onto my face. My friends' glum, worried faces were evident just behind the paramedics and behind them were a motley assortment of onlookers, whispering and gossiping. Before I closed my eyes again, I was convinced that I saw something bright yellow.

Maybe I was dreaming or maybe I imagined it. There are no petals in the wood, I thought.

I did tell the police that I believed it was either Zoe or Paul that had done it, but they didn't believe me. Someone had whacked me on the back of the head with a hitherto unidentified object, that much was certain, but they said that, unless I had actually seen the perpetrators, there was no proof. It was even implied that maybe I had just fallen, drunk, and banged my own head on the stony ground.

I was in hospital, in my own room, although I would have preferred to be in a shared space. Alone, I felt vulnerable. I even asked the police to place a guard by my door but they just looked at me in a sympathetic way and then exchanged a glance over my head. One man and one woman. They were both older than me, maybe in their thirties. The man was bald and portly and the woman was plain. They weren't very friendly to me. I think they even might have thought that I was inventing it all. Particularly as I was not badly hurt at all really. The only reason I was being kept in overnight was because I'd sustained a brief concussion. It made me furious that the police didn't believe me. My friends did, of course. They were allowed to come in to visit one at a time, very briefly, as it was really late by then. Only because, I suspect, I was so agitated that the nurses thought my friends may be able to calm me down. They hadn't seen anything and they were so drunk that their memories couldn't really be relied upon. Julian thought that he may have seen a slim figure running into the wood as he exited the bar but his account was sketchy and uncertain. I wanted it to be either Zoe or Paul but he wouldn't be drawn.

"I don't think that I saw yellow hair, no, I really don't think so."

But I was still convinced, convinced that they were out to get me. Zoe instigated the chain of events in Mexico and here, in this rural idyll, she was determined to finish me off. The police listened to me courteously, with various degrees of patience flickering across their faces. They sat by the hospital bed with notebooks resting in their laps, the male would take notes in tiny writing so I couldn't see. He told me that the main issue was that there was no proof, but that it would be kept as an open investigation until further proof could be unearthed. I spent the night fast asleep in the hospital, I think that they had given me something to help me sleep. In the morning when I woke, my mum and dad were both there. They were sitting side by side holding hands and worry was etched onto their faces.

"Hi love!" said dad, "They couldn't get hold of us straight away because we weren't at home."

I stared at him, uncomprehendingly, he was trying to stifle a grin.

"We went on an overnight theatre trip to the West End!"

In spite of it all, I was happy for them, for my dad in particular. Going to a show and staying overnight in a hotel was definitely my mum's idea of a good time and something which she had always tried to cajole my dad into doing. He used to make excuses not to, he was never into theatre in any form. I realised, now that I knew the whole story, that it was probably a subconscious reaction at her failed attempts at acting. Now, obviously, he'd agree to anything to get back with her. I watched the affectionate way that they sat together, closely touching, and I wondered what had made my mother relent. Had she decided that she loved him after all, or that love was irrelevant when everything else stacked up?

"We've come to take you home love." she said softly, reaching for my hand.

"That's great, thanks, but I have two more exams to do"

"Can't you get out of them, given the circumstances?" mum asked

"No, not really." The truth was that I probably could have got out of them now, if I had tried, but both exams were in my strongest subjects and most likely to drag up my miserable average score.

Also, there was the murky sense of something unresolved. I couldn't leave without proving who had hit me. It had to be sorted out so that I could return in the Autumn, with a clean slate, unencumbered.

"Ok, if you're sure." sighed my dad, "We'll find a local B&B somewhere for a few days until you finish your exams."

They drove me back to my accommodation. I felt normal, practically, just a slight ache at the back of my head. The nurse had given me a couple of leaflets. I glanced at them in the car. One was about counselling and the other about various psychiatric conditions common in teens. I ripped them up surreptitiously and shoved the bits of paper into my pockets. My flatmates welcomed me back with open arms. They all looked worried and extremely exhausted. My role as invalid was reinstated. I lay around for a few days, with my books open beside me, doing the bare minimum. My parents came to see me every day for a few hours and both they and my flatmates scurried around bringing me snacks and cups of tea and treating me as if I was fragile.

I felt a rage expand in me as I sat around. A rage and a pounding in my head near the wound, like a blood vessel was going to shatter. I should have been focussing on my revision but I couldn't relax, couldn't stop thinking. I turned it round and round in my head. It was as if I could see it all very clearly now; the chain of events leading up to this moment. It was all Zoe's doing. Everything that had happened to me was her fault. All done out of some kind of warped jealousy or resentment. She had somehow instigated the attack in Mexico and now, here too, she was the perpetrator. I paced up and down, a violence within me. A brilliant sun was glaring outside, egging me on. Deedee and Carrie were out and Julian was in his room with the door shut. Often, he wore headphones anyway, he was always listening to music. I had been in my pyjamas for days but now I got dressed. I could barely focus on finding clothes or on putting them on. My head was pounding with images. I felt jittery. I was a rabid dog. I threw on what I could find; jeans, a grubby t-shirt from the floor, trainers without socks. I crept out, shutting the door with a gentle click and marched straight over to Zoe's accommodation block.

The main door was unlocked but I did not know which of the twelve flats she lived in. I tried to tone down my fury and approach the task methodically. I knocked on both flats on the ground floor and asked for Zoe. Nobody answered in one. A boy, half asleep, opened the door when I knocked at the other one. He said he didn't know her but then I gave a description. It was fortunate that her hair was as glaring and noticeable as it was. Nevertheless, there was no joy on the ground floor, he still didn't know. However, the girl who answered the door on the first floor, bespectacled, harried, directed me to a flat on the second flat.

"I'm sure that someone with yellow hair lives there..." she mused, and then shut the door, quite rudely I thought. I stood there for a moment breathing deeply and then walked up the next flight of stairs. I felt myself start shaking. I was a lion stalking his prey. My hackles were raised but I had to pretend that nothing was amiss.

Amazingly, it was Paul who answered the door. He just stared at me without saying anything. I realised in that instant, how weak and unthreatening he was.

"I'm sorry you were attacked." he said solemnly, sounding sincere. I ignored him. I could barely hear him above the noise of the blood pounding in my ears.

"Where's Zoe?" I asked trying to keep my tone neutral.

"She's studying I think."

He hadn't invited me in but I pushed past him. Behind me, on the stairs a couple of boys jogged down, laughing. Zoe's room smelt of unwashed clothes and incense, just like mine, only it was neater. There weren't piles of clothes and books on the floor. The bed was made and her desk was uncluttered. She had headphones on but she turned as I entered.

"Er, hi…" she stuttered. She looked shocked and a bit afraid. I could hear my heart still and it wouldn't slow down.

"Let's go for a walk." It was an effort to speak, I could barely hear myself.

She didn't say anything, just looked at me. Clearly, she didn't want to do anything with me but I must have looked as if 'no' wasn't an option.

"Ok." she said bravely, tentatively, her eyes wide.

She sat on her bed and with obvious reluctance, started pulling on her trainers. I shoved my shaking hands into my pockets and waited.

Chapter 31

We walked through the woods to the river. The route was my choice and it felt humid now. The bright sun was obscured by a haze. I marched on ahead, my vision blurry with rage and Zoe stumbled along behind. The clouds hung low. I felt sweat trickling down my back and sticky under my arms. I remembered briefly that I hadn't thought to apply deodorant and then I thought how weird it is to think of mundane matters at a time like this! She chattered all the way, about her course, about Penbridge, even about Emma, but I wasn't listening. All I could hear was my rabid heart and the ferocity of my anger. I focussed on not tripping. I stared at the ground. If I turned, I could see her bright yellow hair bobbing through the shadows of the great trees and through the lush green foliage, like a beacon. I thought, there are no petals in the woods. It was her all along. As we got closer the river called to me, burbling and gurgling. A cacophony of churning water, pretty and ruthless, just like me.

I could tell that she was nervous. She didn't know what I wanted from her. I wouldn't have been able to articulate what I wanted either but when I saw the river, I just knew. She kept chatting and chatting. It was irritating me. It was like the buzz of a mosquito in my ear constantly. My head kept hurting and hurting which was, of course, her fault. In the distance, I could hear the voices of other students. I tried to steer us in the opposite direction. I didn't want to see anyone. I didn't want anyone to see me and stop me.

We got to the water's edge, that wide watery grave spread before us. She was still talking, like a fool. I looked left and right but there was no one there to bear witness and the beast in me took over. All the fear that I had known, all the fear that I believed that she had caused, directly or indirectly, crystalized into pure hard revenge. I pushed her backwards towards the water. She stumbled but didn't fall so I pushed her again. This time she fell backwards with a short, shocked scream and then the water claimed her and pushed her head under and held it there. She had stopped talking finally and I felt peace. Like white water rafting without the raft, I thought. Nobody came and I walked back through the woods, the way that I had come. My mind was clear. I felt washed, purified by relief. My anger had finally disintegrated. My heart stilled and empty.

I walked back to the flat steadily, normally. Sitting there, large and incongruous at the kitchen table, were the same two police officers who had come to see me in hospital. Dee was leaning on the counter and Julian was sitting, twitchily, opposite them and he jumped up when he saw me.

"Where were you? I thought you were in your room!"

"Oh, I just went for a walk, it's such a lovely day!" I smiled airily, but I could smell my own sweat stinking around us and all three of them looked bemused, concerned and suspicious.

"Please sit down." said the man seriously. I sat down. I noticed that they all had mugs of tea. That relaxed me and I grinned. I knew for certain that this couldn't be anything to do with Zoe, it was far too soon.

"Do you mind having your friends here, Abby?" asked the man. I shook my head.

"This morning," continued the portly one, "Someone handed himself into the station. He confessed."

I stared at him. The others looked jubilant but I was confused. Who was it? Paul? Had I attacked the wrong sibling?

"Who?" I asked.

The lady police officer stared hard at me then, as if she was staring right through me. I still felt the river gushing in my ears.

"Ben Davis." she said very clearly and in her voice was an accusation.

"Ben!" I whispered, inside I started sinking. "How?"

She stared down at her police issue notepad. It was plain black. She flicked through it and started reading.

"He drove up from London with someone called Paul? Do you know him?"

I nodded mutely, of course, they still worked together. They must be buddies now, allies.

"Is that Zoe's brother?" asked Dee, he voice animated. I thought, this must be so exciting for them but they were like background extras, I had forgotten that they were there.

"Ben made a statement." continued the woman who didn't like me. Soon she would have cause to like me even less.

"He said that he was very jealous and had taken a bad batch of pills. He talked about where he got them from for a while, and then he went on to say, that he started thinking and he believed that you needed to be taught a lesson and, I quote 'brought down a peg or two'.

The police officer agreed with Ben I could tell and they were both probably right, I realised that then. She looked at me and I said, again, faintly, "Ben?"

I didn't trust myself to say anything else. Julian looked at me with a serious expression, (Deedee looked gleeful still. As if this was a soap opera played out for her entertainment.)

"Where is he now?" Julian asked for my benefit. Because, really, he didn't know me.

"We detained him in custody and we will be transferring him to his home town. Because he mentioned something about hearing voices, there will likely be a mental health assessment of some kind before we can decide what to do with him."

"Will Abby have to see him?" continued Julian

The man looked at me kindly.

"Oh no dear, you won't have to see him. Your nightmare is over." he looked as if he was about to reach over and pat me on the shoulder but then changed his mind.

They got up to leave. The female police officer was still staring at me. There was something unreadable in her expression.

"Is there something you'd like to tell us Abby, before we go?" she looked at me expectantly.

"No." I whispered. The river clamouring still in my head.

"I think that she's in shock." said Julian firmly and saw them out.

I never got to do my final two exams.

I still feel upset about that. I wanted to prove that I could do it. It was important to me. I had never felt clever enough. Zoe's body washed up on the bank of the river by a field and was found by a dog walker, or more specifically by the dog, a Labrador. She had been in the water for several days by then and she was bloated. I imagine that her yellow hair floated like exotic seaweed. Maybe that is what attracted the dog. I think of it bounding down the river bank towards the water's edge, playful and exuberant. The idea of it, the image, brings to me a great sadness. See, I am not all bad.

No one had seen me with Zoe at the river bank, I had made certain of that at the time. However, obviously, several witnesses could attest to seeing me at her accommodation block, searching for her. I was so stupid. Paul, too, saw me cajole her into going for a walk when she didn't want to. Had Ben been in the flat then too? Had he heard me? Did he realise what I was up to? No, that was fanciful. He was probably stoned out of his head, comatose somewhere. Maybe the police had already taken him by then, but wouldn't Zoe or Paul have told me?

I was the only suspect.

It was the same two police officers who came for me. I swear that the woman was smiling to herself, a secret little smile. I could just imagine her turning to her colleagues at the station or to her more trusting partner and gloating;

"I knew that there was something not quite right about that girl. I knew that she was no good." she would go on to boast about her instincts. I recalled then, that people used to say the same about me when I was a child. I could practically hear the conversation as it was happening in my head. There she was then, in front of me, smiling with that particular smugness which comes from being right. The man, however, looked disappointed, as if I had let him down. Deedee let them in and then looked confused when they didn't want to have a cup of tea. They stood straight backed in our kitchen, looking taller than before and more important. They seemed to fill all the available space and Dee hovered, uncertain, not excited this time but concerned. I came out of my room and stood on the other side of the kitchen table. I was dressed and ready, deodorant on, teeth brushed. I stuck my chin in the air.

"Do you know why we are here?" asked the man, sadly.

I nodded. The woman cleared her throat and began;

"Abby Fitzpatrick, we are arresting you…."

I stopped listening, there was a song in my head, something I had heard on the radio years ago, it went like this;

"Tonight, you're mine completely, you give your love so sweetly…"

It went on and on and that's all that I could hear. I could see Dee, my friend, my good friend, out of the corner of my eye. She was standing with her mouth wide open, like a cartoon figure, in total shock.

In any other situation it would have been funny and we would have laughed.

Chapter 32

Dear Abby,

You are no longer dear to me, of course, but I don't know how else to start this letter. I have been writing you letters in my head all of my life, but I never imagined that I would be writing one like this. I hope this even reaches you. I hear they are keeping you in a psychiatric unit until your trial for murdering my sister. I imagine that's for the safety of the public as well as for your own good. Clearly, you are not well. At least, I hope that you are mentally ill because the only other explanation would be that you are evil and I'm not quite ready to believe that yet. Anyway, I don't know if they allow the mental patients to receive mail…although, in reality, this letter is probably beneficial for my own sanity. Really, I don't care how you feel. I just really wanted to let you know how wrong you were about everything. And, I really mean everything. My sister was entirely innocent. She had such a shitty life and now, because of you, she is dead, and her chance of a better future is buried with her.

The only thing that you were right about was that I was in love with you. All my life. Yes. Ever since I saw you when I was about 9 and you were ten or eleven, and a total princess even then. You were so stuck up and full of yourself, everyone thought that, you just believed that you were better. But I used to think; well, of course! You were better! I used to believe that physical beauty somehow signified that there was also beauty inside…as if the physical bit was somehow just the tip of the iceberg! I was an idiot, I know. Yet my obsession with you endured, I got older and plainer and you just got more and more stunning and unreachable. It wasn't even frustrating for me, no, frustration would have been the normal reaction, but you see, by then, my sister and I had long since given up on positive things happening to us. Our expectations of life were laughably low.

I don't know what, if anything, you can remember about our parents. I know that my mum was even friendly with your mum for a while, she could do that in short bursts, put on a front for the public. It was important for both of them that we never let the mask slip, that we maintain the guise of a normal family. We couldn't really pretend to be happy, of course, our acting was not that accomplished, but we had to pretend to be 'normal' otherwise things would be even worse for us. We cottoned on to that pretty quickly. Once, when we were tiny, I think Zoe was in reception and I was in nursery, Zoe told the teacher that our parents didn't love us, that they were mean to us, and they both got called in to a meeting with the Head and Zoe's teacher. Of course, they managed to wangle their way out of it. They put on their super smiley, concerned faces and pretended to laugh, even, and shook their heads dolefully and my mum told them that my sister had always had such a wild imagination! Also, there were lots of films at the time about mistreated kids and that kind of thing helped my parents as they could just say that Zoe was relating the plot of a film. Not that we ever went to the cinema, and our punishment was such on that occasion, that neither Zoe nor I ever tried to get another adult involved again.

I believe, that after that particular incident, we were locked into our separate bedrooms without food or water for 24 hours. That was a favourite punishment of theirs, applicable after any alleged misdemeanour. The advantage of it, from their point of view, was that no marks were left on the body, ergo, no evidence. We were weak and sickly, yes, but so were a lot of children back then. We didn't really stand out. They did hit us too but they tended to avoid noticeable places. They were smart, they rarely left marks.

Because we were sporadically starved, my sister developed a complex relationship with food. She would steal chocolate bars when she could and stuff them down… she craved sugar above all else. I guess chocolate, so I have read, is supposed to replicate love and obviously, that's what we were lacking. We had none of that. Bulimia, I think they call it. Anyway, she had an awful time of it, worse than me in many ways. I don't know if it was because she was older or because she was a girl, but my parents used to goad her continuously about being ugly and stupid. More so than me. They weren't great to me either, but I didn't care about the 'ugly' taunt, and she really did. She had you and Emma as friends!

She wasn't responsible for what happened to you in Mexico. I have no idea how your brain made that leap, but it is extremely far-fetched. It was Emma and Enrique if anyone! She wasn't even there!

The worst thing about all of it, was that she was so excited to be going to university and to be getting away from our parents. She had to work so hard, she was starved, she had a miserable, abusive home life and she wasn't naturally bright like you and Emma were. She got to Penbridge and she finally felt free and for the first time ever, as if she had a future.

She didn't understand why you were so weird with her. She felt sorry for you.

I wish I had stopped her from going on that walk with you that day. It will haunt me forever. Even then, I was blinded by lust for you.

 Seems like your looks turned out to be more of a curse than a blessing, for all of us.

Paul

Epilogue

My name is Abby.

I am not pretty anymore.

I keep my hair so short that it is practically shaved and I don't do it in a cool way. I do it because I don't care. I am serving ten years for manslaughter. They tell me that I may be released after five years, for good behaviour. I'm not sure if my behaviour is good. It is nothing mainly. They keep me heavily medicated and sedated. Through the small high window, I see bars and pigeons. Sometimes feathers flutter in like gifts. I consider them gifts. I watch soap operas on a small TV. This place is better than my previous cell in Mexico. This one is cleaner. There is a proper toilet. But I do not have a cellmate. I am not allowed to have anyone here with me because I am considered to be too unstable. I miss Penny. One day, when I get my thoughts together in one place, I will write to her. I will tell her that I miss watching the Mexican soap operas with her. I miss the way that she would translate for me, the important bits and there were lots of important bits. I even miss sleeping next to her and sharing the bottles of water. I miss having someone else's smell near me. Here it smells sterile, of bleach.

The jail is in my home town which is fortunate. My mum and dad come to visit me every week. They sit opposite me, on the other side of a table. We are not allowed to touch in case they try to smuggle something in to me. I don't know what. I don't want anything anymore. My parents are back together again. My mum is living at home but she no longer looks glamourous. Her hair is nearly entirely grey and she doesn't bother dyeing it or wearing make-up anymore. She looks older than she should. Dad looks very sad and defeated and bemused often, as if he still can't quite believe it.

The only positive outcome is that Caitlin left my brother as soon as she heard about my crime. She didn't want to be tethered to any family which could harbour within it such evil.

Printed in Great Britain
by Amazon